TO WATCH A GIANT FALL

C. S. ALFONSO

To Mom and Dad,
for raising me to be curious

Who sees the snowflake
When an avalanche tears down the mountainside
Swallowing you in a flurry of white

Who hears the *tink* of a pebble
When an earthquake rumbles
Chasms the ground until you stumble

Who feels the kiss of a droplet
When a flood sweeps you away
Pulls you beneath hungry waves

Who smells the promise of spring
When fire fills the air with smoke
Chokingly thick, a harsh yoke

Who tastes golden spices
When betrayal stings
Metallic like blood, and vengeance rings

Oh, to watch a giant fall

PROLOGUE

Lights flickered dark throughout the empire, as though a sweeping wind was covering the land in a blanket of shadow. Candles sputtered out and hearths lost their glow.

Osandit could see all this from the highest balcony of the Grand Palace. One moment, a thousand lights glimmered like stars over the hilly terrain, and the next, he could hardly discern the outline of his capital city. And if he were to ride out past the barrier, he knew what he would find: a hundred lightless towns stretching as far as the Verinian Sea.

No wind could claim responsibility for this shadow. Only Osandit could—he and the imperious hand of tradition were to blame. Tonight marked the final night of mourning. After he took his vows at sunset tomorrow, the empire would cease this senseless practice.

Despite his sheltered upbringing, Osandit wasn't stupid—not a single soul in the empire actually mourned his parents' deaths. Certainly not the shopkeeper who'd been forced to turn over an outlandish percentage of profits to fund the army, nor the parents who'd lost their eldest to the war overseas. Not even Osandit could honestly admit to missing his parents. They were monsters falling into their own greed and taking the empire down with them.

Which was precisely why Osandit had killed them. Not directly, of course. If the Council ever investigated the late emperor's death and found Osandit guilty, he would lose the throne as quickly as he'd secured it. But the trail would never lead back to him; besides, the Council's chairwoman had given him the idea in the first place.

Exhaustion finally sinking in, Osandit turned from the balcony and locked the door behind him. The chill of a fireless room in the dead of winter forced him to don many uncomfortable layers of fur, and he had yet to grow accustomed to sleeping in them. Tomorrow, that would change.

Tomorrow, everything would change.

It took hours to prepare for the coronation. Osandit spent the better part of the early morning rehearsing the ceremony until the chairwoman declared his performance satisfactory and sent him off to the clothier. The sheer effort it took for the apprentice to affix the ornamental armor around his torso convinced Osandit to slip a few extra coins into the boy's pocket.

By the end, Osandit's head pounded and his feet ached from holding his weight, and that of the oppressive shining armor, up for so long. Though, as Osandit sat on the Crown Prince's throne for the last time, gazing out the yawning crystal windows, he welcomed the pain. Such a small price for what was to come, for what he would do.

The Inami queen's ship should have docked two hours ago, and the carriage Osandit had sent would be halfway back to the palace by now. The monarch's very presence in his empire made history—and the treaty they would sign on the eve of his coronation would mark the first between their nations since the War of Pasos. The swoop of a pen—able to spare so many lives, nurse an empire back to life.

"Your Majesty," a lilting voice called from the entrance.

Slowly, because that voice could never startle him, Osandit's eyes abandoned the windows for a much greater prize. Teliah stood under the throne room's arched entrance, emerald eyes glittering amusedly. At his smile, she drifted to him, each step as graceful as the spirit after which her people were named. She wore a dress the color between blush and violet that peeked out when the sun kissed the horizon, rare and beautiful, just like its bearer.

"My love," Osandit finally whispered when she reached his throne. An infectious smile touched Teliah's face. He'd never said that before, aloud, in a space where anyone might walk in at any moment and hear it.

Instead of responding, Teliah reached out a hand and laced her fingers through his. A tapestry of light and dark, their joined hands made Osandit the happiest man in the world. For that simple gesture, his parents would have stripped him of his honors, and done much worse to Teliah. And unlike the war, many of his people would agree with that sentiment—something they would fix, in time, together.

Teliah gently untangled her fingers from his and wandered to the empress's throne. She flattened her palm atop the smooth golden armrest, admiring the contact. "I think I'll look quite regal on this," she commented innocently.

Osandit couldn't hide his grin. "I expect no less from you, *Your Highness*."

Teliah returned to his throne and lifted herself to perch on the armrest. If it weren't for her height and able miner's muscles, she would have looked silly. Gazing down at her emperor, she tentatively reached her hand to the side of his face.

"Are you ready?"

"I am," Osandit said. He meant it.

As the sun set behind the palace, the High Vera lowered the glimmering crown onto the new emperor's head. The crowd below the veranda exploded into cheers.

"Verali is with our King," the High Vera announced over the noise.

With that, Osandit rose from his knees.

The temple leader's face contorted in annoyance at the hoots and whistles. Traditionally, the High Vera conducted this ceremony in the temple beneath the palace, away from the dirt of the streets and the stench of the poor. But Osandit had insisted, arguing that a public coronation would send a stronger message and quell the dissent that had spread like disease during his parents' reign.

To his right, the Inami queen clapped politely, the iridescent sleeves of her gown billowing in the wind. The Crown Princess of Inam clapped, too, but the slight downturn of her lips reminded Osandit why he'd had to rush this.

The queen had lost her youth decades ago, and Osandit's father had received word from his spies that the Inami Council had begun preparing for the Crown Princess to take over. Where the current queen sought peace, the princess craved vengeance. Osandit didn't blame her—the senseless war started by his father over a trading post had razed many Inami towns and crippled their economy.

While Queen Lorion held no love for Verinia nor its late rulers, she'd agreed to a treaty the moment Osandit's letter arrived at her desk. No bloodshed, a small sum of reparations to rebuild her queendom, and the war would end. If the princess had her say, she'd have rejected any attempt at peace and sent her army instead. An eye for an eye, one broken nation for another.

The plaza's cheers washed away Osandit's thoughts as he bowed to his people. When he turned around, his heart fluttered. Teliah, as beautiful and fierce as ever, stood in a small sea of nobles who steadfastly ignored her presence. She stared at Osandit with all the reverence in the world.

His company retreated into the palace, but not before Osandit gave his people a wave that spoke louder than any contrived speech could have. One last roar of the crowd before the gilded doors closed behind him, snuffing out the noise.

The two rulers walked through the palace halls to his study, an entourage of Verinian and Inami nobility in tow. On his desk sat the treaty and two plain quills freshly dipped in ink.

Once the queen signed, Osandit's Chief Advisor stepped forward. "Do you, your Royal Majesty, Queen Lorion the Third of Inam, pledge to this agreement for you and your royal blood that may follow?"

Osandit couldn't help but glance at the disgruntled princess as her mother pledged away her right to war.

His hand didn't tremble when he wrapped his fingers around the pen.

"Do you, your Royal Majesty, Emperor Osandit the First of Verinia, pledge to this agreement for you and your royal blood that may follow?"

"I do."

With that, the Master of War left to call back his troops and send notices to the drafted soldiers and their families.

———

Alone in his room, Osandit stared at the twinkling lights that traveled up and down the hills of his land, and with a tired inhale, contemplated his reign.

Tonight every town would receive word that the war was over, that their sons and daughters could return home. Celebrations would ensue, and during Osandit's royal tour he would witness firsthand his changed empire.

Everything—

A sharp wave of light pierced through the night sky. Osandit frowned, searching his memory for an upcoming solar event. Nothing stood out to him. Surely, the astronomers would have mentioned it, whatever it was.

Not a few seconds after these thoughts passed through his head, Osandit heard the first explosion. Saw it, too. One moment, the lights of a town blinked tranquilly. The next, a raging fire tore through every house in the Grand Valley.

Osandit didn't speculate. He didn't wonder if this was an Inami attack, whether he had judged the queen wrong, or whether the princess didn't respect the treaty.

No, there was no time to think of that.

The second explosion sounded, a third following quickly after. It was a noise that deafened, clawing into Osandit's ears like a rabid animal.

Still in his nightclothes, Osandit flew out of his chambers and sprinted through the halls, ignoring any noble or advisor trying to flag him down. The only thought running through his mind was *Teliah*.

Get to her, his mind screamed. *Find her and flee.*

Osandit prayed that she hadn't left for a midnight stroll through the city. That an assassin hadn't slipped into her bedroom and slit her throat in some twisted form of revenge against him.

He couldn't get the image out of his mind, as if it had already happened: blood, her lifeless eyes—

"Osandit!"

There she was, standing before him in a simple white gown, black hair a mess. He wrapped her in a tight embrace, only letting go when she pushed against him.

"We must leave," she declared. "Come, let us find Illian and call for a carriage."

So brave. "I thought…"

"I know, Osandit, I know," she whispered the words like a lullaby. She stroked his hair with a gentle hand. "Where would Illian be?"

The question plucked Osandit from his trance. "The shelters."

The shelters were a system of caverns that snaked underneath the palace. They began at the highest level with the High Vera's temple, then burrowed further into the ground—the depths were reserved for the nobility and royal family during an emergency. But the shelters dated back to a Verinia before the War of Pasos, when the nobility was a third of what it was now. The food in the reserves wouldn't last two weeks even if they fasted intermittently.

Out of the corner of his eye, Osandit swore he could see a shadowed figure in the distance, but it disappeared before he could be sure. He kept pace with his betrothed, which Osandit attributed to the training his parents had subjected him to as a boy and which he'd kept up as an adult. Teliah's agility was natural—the product of a bloodline always fighting to survive.

They reached the entrance to the shelters in a matter of minutes: a staircase that wound down for ages, hidden behind a tapestry of Verali. Osanti pulled back the muted depiction of the empire's deity with some aggression, yellow and orange fabric rippling like fire.

Another explosion reached their ears, closer this time.

Where are you now? Osandit wanted to scream at the god. *Where are you while your people die?* But this wasn't Verali—just colored ropes woven together in his image. Tapestries didn't answer prayers.

Teliah tugged on his forearm, leading Osandit into the shelters. The staircase was clean enough when they began—dirtless, the occasional ceiling web the servants didn't bother to reach. But once they passed the temple, more moss touched their boots than stone, and dust filled their lungs. Osandit let out a sigh of relief when the stairs released them into the shelters.

The sigh caught in his throat when he saw it. He choked.

Blood... blood everywhere—on the walls, on the bodies... on the ceiling.

"We must go," Osandit heard Teliah say. But he couldn't move, feet frozen in place. "We will get the carriage ourselves," she said, pulling his arm harder.

Yes, Osandit thought. They would have to, because the slumped body of his favorite advisor surely wouldn't.

Teliah eventually managed to wrest Osandit from his stupor and drag him back into the staircase. On their way up, they slipped into the temple to retrieve weapons.

"An assassin must have infiltrated the palace," Osandit said as he handed Teliah one of the temple's two ceremonial swords. They were sacred pieces used in the temple's rituals, and hadn't felt the metallic tang of blood in centuries.

Perhaps now they finally would.

An assassin... But Osandit couldn't shake the feeling that this was bigger than him. Some of the explosions had sounded too far away.

They made their way to leave when a muffled groan stopped them. Osandit held a finger to his mouth. Teliah nodded, lips pressed in a grim line.

The High Vera's temple was made of orange clay to honor Verali's fire. The raised platform they currently stood on overlooked rows of dark wood benches. Osandit had spent much of his childhood sitting on those benches listening to the High Vera. A man with such passion and hollowness, such love and hate, that being in his presence gave Osandit whiplash; he walked away from every encounter with the impression he would never be able to fully trust the temple leader.

But for all his hesitations, Osandit didn't hate the man, and a pang of sadness hit him when he stepped into the preacher's private chambers. Laying atop his bed, limbs contorted and bloodied, the High Vera's face scared Osandit more than he would ever admit.

Osandit tenderly closed the High Vera's eyes.

Teliah approached the source of the groaning. She threw open the closet door to reveal the Inami queen and princess splayed on the floor.

The princess's eyes fluttered open. Sweat and blood covered her face like specks of paint. "You..." she groaned. Her fingers tightened around a dagger coated in some black substance. "I cut your demon," she gritted out, each breath a battle.

"What dem—"

It all happened so fast. The princess lurched forward, shoving the dagger into Osandit's calf. He cried out as pain laced through his leg.

The princess collapsed into her dead mother's lap.

Blood ran down the blade of the dagger: Osandit's red, and the demon's black.

Teliah ripped the High Vera's robe into a makeshift bandage and wrapped it around Osandit's wound. Then, with his arm slung across her shoulders, they climbed the last stretch of stairs. They stayed in the shadows on their way to the carriage house, hoping to avoid whatever demon had painted the shelters in blood.

With each passing minute, Osandit's pain became harder to bear. When they found a carriage, Osanti collapsed inside while Teliah went to find a horse.

Osandit peered at his wound and sucked in a quick breath. Around the dagger's mark, a bright red rash spread up his thigh, and his veins ran an unnaturally dark purple.

Poison.

As far as Osandit knew, the palace's weapons master didn't use this type of poison. It was rare, harvested from wiltflower pollen, a plant found only in the mountainous regions of Inam. Which meant... it meant that the princess had brought it in herself.

She had planned to kill him, break the treaty—and the war would continue.

His reign had been damned from the start.

All around him, blasts rang out. Osandit peered out the carriage window down at the Grand Valley. Bright orange flames reflected in his eyes. Fire danced, raging, consuming. It left nothing behind but ash and death.

Osandit wondered if this chaos had anything to do with the demon the princess spoke of. The Inami didn't have the resources to launch an attack of this magnitude; if they did, they would have done this earlier in the war. No, this was someone else—*something* else.

A horse's neigh announced Teliah's arrival. She led two brown mares to the front of the carriage. Once she finished fastening the horses' reins, she spoke to Osandit through the window.

"There are no riders."

"None? But..." Understanding dawned on Osandit. "Dead?" he asked, though he already knew the answer by the look on Teliah's face.

She nodded as she mounted one of the horses. "The bodies were fresh, Osandit."

A tremor of fear rang in her voice.

She was right to be afraid. As the horses nickered and drew the carriage forward, a glinting arrow tore through the night. Osandit heard the wet thud of a body hitting the mud and bones cracking. The horses whined and galloped faster.

"Teliah!"

Osandit leaned out of the carriage, the poison making his movements lethargic. "Stop!" he yelled at the horses, but they didn't speak his language. Without a rider, they spoke instincts, and right now everything was telling them to run.

Stupidly, Osandit unclasped the lock on the door and tumbled out of the carriage. He landed painfully. Dizzy from the fall and the poison, he staggered to the dead body beside the carriage tracks.

The moon illuminated Teliah's face, her wide, haunted eyes silver under its light. His gaze flitted to the metal jutting from her abdomen and the blood pooling around the wound.

He fell to his knees. "Teliah," he whispered, cupping the side of her face. "Teliah!"

When she didn't respond, lifeless eyes staring at nothing, Osandit let out a strangled sob.

By the time the demon found him, Osandit had already died in every way that mattered. His kingdom was destroyed, his lover killed. For all his sense of righteousness, Osandit wasn't a fighter. He didn't challenge the cloaked figure that neared him with a blade.

A hood obscured the demon's face until it was standing directly over him. Pure white eyes stared down at him, eyes that were not of this world.

"What are you?"

A voice infiltrated his thoughts, low and gravely. *The fall*, it said.

Of what? Osandit wanted to ask.

Of everything, the voice rasped inside his head, before cutting it off.

PART 1

THE GIANT

CHAPTER 1

6 MONTHS PRIOR
EARTH

Everybody agreed that Henry Carter had chosen a terrible time to leave the womb.

On the thirtieth of March, in a cold wing of the Dartmouth-Hitchcock hospital, a healthy baby boy named Henry opened his eyes for the first time. And cried. Henry cried a lot.

His mother Helen cried a lot, too. She held the tiny, dark-red human in her arms as hot tears streamed down her face. Her husband Evan, Henry's father, sat on a faux leather chair in the corner of the labor room and watched his wife.

Dark circles lined Evan's eyes. He took a sip of the tepid black hospital coffee in his hand. Having Henry had been Helen's idea. She said she needed the baby to move on. Evan didn't, but if Henry was what it took to keep Helen from breaking down every time it came up...

Here they were, crying and exhausted with an hour-old Henry.

Near the entrance of the hospital in another of those faux leather chairs, freezing from the New Hampshire weather, Elaine contemplated her brother's birth. She stomped the snow off her boots and silently thanked the hospital's heating system as her shivering eased.

Elaine knew the reason behind Helen's sudden desire to be pregnant, and she hated it. Because while everyone forgot, she would remember. She would carry this weight with her for the rest of her life. No baby could take that away.

Yet when Elaine finally held her brother in her arms, crying and all, love swelled in her chest. Which made her even more frustrated, because—as everybody agreed—Henry Carter had chosen a terrible time to be born.

Nobody blamed Helen or Evan; nine months ago the news hadn't broken yet. And nobody blamed Henry either, for obvious reasons.

There was no one to blame for a baby born during the end of the world.

CHAPTER 2

PRESENT DAY

If someone had told Elaine a year ago that she would willingly allow a stranger to drive her to an undisclosed location high in the mountains, she would have laughed in their face.

But here she was.

Her breath fogged the car window. She leaned against the glass, watching the trees pass. The road cut this forest in half, a concrete chasm at its heart. The animals hadn't yet learned to avoid it; two gray foxes stared curiously at Elaine from a few feet away.

The sun was sliding below the horizon, coloring the sky twilight. Elaine observed the purples, oranges and pinks swirling like watercolors, but she could not appreciate the view. Apprehension wound around her chest like a venomous snake. She didn't know where she was or where she was going. The driver had abandoned roads with any sort of directional signs hours ago. All Elaine had to go on was that he had left her house going north, so they should be somewhere in Vermont by now. If he hadn't changed direction along the way without her noticing. Which very well could have been the case.

The driver, a middle-aged man with dark brown hair cropped close to his scalp, had appeared at Elaine's doorstep early this morning, just as the invitation had said he would. Elaine did not know his name. They had gotten into the car without so much as a word exchanged, Elaine's parents watching from the doorstep.

Elaine could still see the image in her mind: Helen and Evan with Henry in his arms, huddled together on the patio, staring at her with twin expressions of dread and hope. A strange combination, but then again, these were strange times.

The road transitioned from concrete to gravel, the gritty crunch a welcome distraction from her anxious thoughts. Soon after they abandoned the paved road, a fog penetrated the forest. It curled in whisps, reaching from the trees, shifting indeterminately. In seconds it became impossible to see through.

Elaine half-expected Lily to break through the fog, for her to run out of the trees in that blue dress seared into Elaine's memory. But as eerie as the forest seemed, Elaine doubted it housed ghosts.

Besides, this wasn't even the same woods her sister had died in.

Elaine shook her head and banished thoughts of Lily. She needed to arrive level-headed, smart and ready for the trials. Not a bawling mess still grieving over the death of her sister. From what little the invitation had divulged, Elaine understood her intelligence would be tested, her limits pushed, and that there was a strong chance she wouldn't qualify for the Defense.

The letter had been sitting in their mailbox when they returned home from the hospital with Henry. A navy envelope with a gold wax seal pressed into the shape of a bee held the parchment. Elaine remembered that Evan was frantically calling bunker groups, trying to find one they could afford, when Elaine had brought him the letter.

Dear Elaine Carter, it read in a delicate cursive hand.

This letter is to inform you that you have been selected to participate in a round of trials to determine the youth division of our defense strategy. Should you pass these trials, you will be invited to aid in the defense of your country, and of the world. In exchange for your service, your family will be offered a place in the National Bunker.

The next paragraph contained the details of entering the trials and when she would leave home—along with a warning not to share the contents of the letter with anyone, or else have the offer revoked.

When they had read over the invitation in disbelief, Helen and Evan looked as though they'd been given the greatest gift in the world, never mind that they might lose their only daughter.

But since Lily's death, Elaine's relationship with her parents had deteriorated until they barely spoke. Perhaps they wouldn't miss her. Perhaps they were even happy to trade their adopted daughter for a newborn son.

Elaine wondered if she would ever see them again. A small part of her missed them already, as fractured as their three-person family had been.

And Henry. Elaine missed Henry dearly, his innocent smiles and cries. If she failed, his eyes might never crinkle in delight again, his face might never bunch up in unbridled curiosity about a world that hadn't yet taught him to fear it. *For Henry*, she swore. For Henry, she would do whatever it took. She would fight.

News of the impending war had broken a few months before Henry's birth. Coverage of the topic was spotty at first, when governments might still have been trying to keep the discovery a secret lest the public erupt into chaos. But by the time Elaine received the letter, almost everyone believed the end of the world was imminent. Individuals and companies began constructing bunkers, and those fortunate enough to afford membership began joining—Elaine's family not among them.

The car approached a rotting stone wall covered in so many vines it almost blended into the forest. Outside Elaine's window, the metal bars of an open gate flew past.

At last, the car came to a stop. Elaine heard the driver's door slam. He opened the door for her and a gust of chilly mountain air pummeled her when she stepped out.

Elaine hadn't known what to expect. The invitation had been vague as to where the trials would take place. But whatever she'd envisioned—a large tower, an office building, barracks of some sort—it wasn't this.

At the very top of the mountain, with fog surrounding the gates like a moat, stood a castle. Alabaster towers stretched into the sky, their sharp tips piercing the overcast. A hundred windows glimmered in the fading sunlight, and two colossal, sword-wielding marble angels guarded the entrance.

The castle's interior was the glorious promise of its exterior: a high glass ceiling let in a soft wash of sunlight and the view of hazy rain clouds, Greek columns lined the room, and a grand staircase rose into a landing that overlooked the entryway. Even minor details, like the designs carved into the copper railings, exuded ancient luxury.

A prickle danced over Elaine's skin, eliciting goosebumps. Her gaze searched the pockets of shadow under the landing, then traveled upwards—there.

A pair of steely eyes studied her from the landing. The boy leaning against the railing couldn't have been much older than she was. Black curls framed his face, fanning over his forehead. He wore a white shirt and black trousers. She couldn't read his expression. What held her attention were his eyes; they were bright blue, stark against dark lashes, the color of the ocean—

He tilted his head ever so slightly when he noticed her staring back. Elaine felt bare under his scrutiny, a vigilant gaze that seemed to miss nothing.

"Leave your bags here," the driver said, tearing her attention away. "They will be delivered to your room later." The entryway echoed his voice as Elaine followed instructions. She set her backpack and duffel onto the gleaming bell cart beside the potted olive tree.

By the time Elaine looked up again, the boy had disappeared. She ignored the twinge of disappointment in her chest and followed the driver to her room.

They walked behind the staircase into a long stretch of hallway. Elaine glanced out the windows at the forest.

She had thought there was something eerie about the spindly trees during the drive. But now, in the fading light, with the forest's stillness and the fog's creeping fingers of gray, Elaine truly believed this mountain was haunted.

From that hallway, Elaine's room was up an enclosed spiral staircase on the third floor and in a small hall that branched out from the main one.

"Thank you," Elaine said to the man after he'd indicated which door was hers.

He only nodded in response, and Elaine wondered if he could sense her unease. She wondered if he even knew about the trials.

Just before turning the corner, the driver stopped to look back at her. "Good luck," he said.

Elaine knew she would need it.

CHAPTER 3

Silence tracked Elaine into her room. Or rather, rooms. The castle's aged layout pushed the actual bedroom behind a sitting room furnished with a sofa, coffee table, and paintings of different landscapes. Elaine paused to study the art.

One painting featured a dark forest, thin trunks spreading into a canopy that blocked all light. Perhaps that was the same woods surrounding the castle.

Another showed a lake under swaths of moonlight, lonely but for a single swan in the center, an ethereal glow about its feathers. Its ebony eyes seemed to be staring back at her through the canvas.

The hinges whined as Elaine pushed open the bedroom door. A four-poster bed was the only furniture. Intricate carvings climbed the glossed wooden pillars like vines, and plush maroon sheets covered the mattress. A bed fit for some ancient noble.

Out the window, she watched the car round the driveway and vanish past the gates.

Elaine drifted to another window that overlooked the manicured lawn. Grass stretched in alternating stripes of lighter green and darker green until it reached the forest. The trees stood like sentinels, quietly watching. A shiver snaked down her spine, even though the window was closed. As the sun dipped below the horizon, the forest looked more like a line of jagged teeth, hungry and waiting to swallow her whole.

She stared until the last of the light had bled from the sky and she heard two raps at the door. Elaine slipped through the sitting room to open it for a plump woman. A plain gray dress hugged the servant's figure, and her white hair was pulled into a tight bun.

"Dinner is being served," the servant said in a high voice that didn't at all match her body. Elaine followed the woman downstairs.

The dining room felt empty, more due to its cavernous size than a lack of people. A group of about fifty sat around the end of one of two long tables. Hushed voices went quiet once they noticed Elaine.

Elaine thanked the servant before turning to study the others. They seemed to be around her age, though one girl couldn't have been older than thirteen. They all had the same look: sharp, calculating eyes and pursed lips. They studied her, too. Wondered whether she would be weak. Whether she would break easily, or if it would take effort to surpass her.

Wolves. Elaine had wandered into a den of starving wolves watering at the mouth. Unfortunately for them, she was just as hungry, just as desperate—if not more. After all, she had a past to atone for, too.

Elaine approached them, pausing to decide where she should sit. Not next to the girl with ink-black hair and a gaze of disdain. Not next to the boy who looked like he wanted to stab her with his fork.

The girl Elaine had noticed earlier, the one who looked far too young to be here, offered a slight smile.

"Is this everyone?" Elaine asked once she had sat down and the chatter resumed.

"No, I don't think so." The girl had a fluttery voice. She tucked a strand of blonde hair behind her ear and added, "That's what everyone's saying. The trials don't start till Friday, so more people are probably coming."

Around a hundred more, if Elaine was estimating the number of seats across the two tables correctly.

"What's your name?" the girl asked.

"Elaine. You?"

"Kate."

The arrival of dinner saved Elaine from uncomfortable silence. Servants laid out trays of mashed potatoes, salad, and meats. Other than the fact they ate in a castle, there was nothing particularly special about their meal. The chicken tasted plain and the salad needed more dressing. But that money was better spent elsewhere, Elaine supposed. The National Bunker wouldn't build itself. Besides, she hadn't come here for the food.

A knife clattered. When Elaine looked up, she found herself under the scrutiny of a harsh, icy gaze. The boy from earlier. He... Well, he wasn't glaring, exactly, but he didn't look happy to see her, either. It wasn't any emotion Elaine could recognize. No, she realized, it wasn't an emotion—his eyes were gears, the working of his mind as he schemed.

She looked away. She hadn't come for the company, either.

Elaine scraped the last of the potatoes off her plate and set her spoon down, ready to leave and catch some sleep.

"We won't have to kill each other, will we?"

Elaine's head snapped up. What little conversations there were stopped abruptly, all eyes on the girl who'd spoken. The girl hadn't sounded afraid, or even reserved. As if she'd been asking if they'd shake hands after dinner or what they should wear for the first trial.

Kill each other? The letter hadn't said anything about *killing.* Elaine wouldn't have come if it had. Evan and Helen wouldn't have let her. But as an echoing quiet set in, Elaine's certainty wavered. She would have come no matter what. Too much was at stake; no price was too high, not her life, and not her morals.

Elaine surveyed the somber faces. They had arrived at the same conclusion she had.

The line of trees drew closer, sentinels marching. But it was Elaine's steps that closed the distance, not the imagined figures. One foot in front of the other until she reached the forest line. Until the trees loomed over her. Their branches rustled in the evening breeze, leaves waving. *Welcome,* they seemed to be saying.

But Elaine didn't feel welcome. The air was cold and the shadows cast by long, skeletal branches were disquieting. And soon, the sun would disappear, dragging her vision below the horizon with it.

Still, she couldn't have stood another second in the castle. Three days in and she'd grown restless. Itching for something to distract her from her thoughts, which tended to revolve around the impending trials, or Lily— neither were pleasant subjects. The library had grown tiresome after the first day when Elaine discovered the only volumes were scientific works or religious tomes. Or books written in some ancient script she couldn't decipher. And other than Kate, Elaine didn't speak to the other competitors.

A path broke through the trees, twisting around dark roots toward the heart of the forest. It hadn't felt the pressure of human feet recently; at times, Elaine could barely tell it apart from the rest of the soil. But the path was entrenched enough in the terrain that Elaine never lost sight of it for more than a few seconds.

Time slipped away, lazily wiping the sky free of dusk. The pinks and purples blurred into the black of night. By the time Elaine reached the end of the path, only a facade of light remained, the rays that lingered longer than they were supposed to. Soon even they would retreat.

Elaine was too focused on the scene in front of her to pay attention to the dimming light or the rustle of leaves. She'd wondered whether the paintings in her room were of this forest. Now she was certain. The artist had captured the lake perfectly: how the tips of pine trees reflected in the water, how the wind cast ripples over the surface, how the water sparkled. Even the swan, though it now drifted near the shore, not in the center as it had been immortalized, was a twin to its painted sister.

Snap. Elaine spun around, now keenly aware of the encroaching darkness. A branch, that had to have been a branch. Only a large animal could have broken one that loudly—or a person. Elaine didn't know which she preferred.

"Hello?"

The forest absorbed her voice, greedy. Sinister. Waiting. In daylight, the trees hid their monsters well. Once the sun set, the darkness let them loose.

"Sorry."

Elaine jumped at the voice. Male, young. Another competitor, then—one whose voice she didn't recognize.

"I didn't mean to scare you," he tried again, stepping out of the shadows.

His cover fell away, revealing sun-kissed hair and warm skin, alluding to many hours spent outside. She recognized him. He'd arrived yesterday.

"What are you doing here?" Her words came out harshly.

"I was..." he hesitated, grappling for the right answer.

She finished the sentence for him. "Following me."

"Well, yes—but only because I was worried you'd get lost or eaten by a bear. I didn't mean to scare you."

"Why didn't you just say something to me earlier?"

He sighed. "I was going to, but you seemed so... concentrated." Before Elaine could respond, he glanced at his watch and said, "We should head back. Dinner'll be starting soon."

Her initial startle faded into a dull hum, and she followed him back to the castle. She suspected, as everyone did, that tonight's dinner would be important, for the trials began tomorrow. As they made their way through the forest, darkness finally fell, and she had to admit it was comforting to have somebody by her side.

"Did you plan on tackling the bear?" Elaine asked as they neared the forest's edge, amusement coloring her tone. The boy picked up on it after a beat of confusion.

He laughed, reaching his arm to rub the nape of his neck. "Honestly, I'm not sure. I just figured two was better odds than one."

The image of them trying to wrestle a grizzly with their bare hands drew a laugh from her. "It would've killed us both."

He agreed with a sheepish grin. "Probably."

The lights from the castle reached halfway across the lawn, and Elaine felt a weight lifting when she crossed into it, like she had escaped the forest's shadowy grasp.

From a distance, the castle seemed quiet, a slumbering relic of the past. Peaceful, even, if a building could be described that way. But the figures moving in the windows and the soft footfalls beside her reminded Elaine the castle was anything but. Tonight, it would feed and shelter them. Tomorrow, the castle would become their battleground. It would test them and bend them and break them to forge an army.

"I didn't catch your name," Elaine prompted.

"Mason." He glanced at her, then averted his gaze to the garden.

A maze of hedges and florals, adorned with statues covered in vines, the garden bridged the gap between lawn and castle. Stepping stones led to the back entrance. They passed under arched greenery, the burbling water from a nearby fountain filling the early evening air with its song.

"I'm Elaine," she replied.

The frosted glass doors at the edge of the garden were unlocked as Elaine had left them, thankfully. If not, they would've had to sprint around the entirety of the castle to make it to dinner on time.

When they reached the dining room, the usual chatter didn't reach her ears. The silence gave Elaine pause. It was laced with trepidation, with the nerves of a crowd waiting to be addressed.

They slipped through the open double doors, and Elaine was surprised to find that nameplates marked each seat. Only a few chairs remained empty, so locating their assigned places didn't take long. Dozens of eyes followed their hasty movements, wondering why they were late, together. Hoping their tardiness foreshadowed a swift elimination.

Elaine studied the cursive lettering of her nameplate, similar to the letter that had called her here. Not more than a month had passed since she'd received that envelope, yet the memory of opening it played back like a scene that belonged to another life. Perhaps it did. Then, she'd had Helen and Evan and Henry—a family, however broken they had been.

Now, she had no one.

Two more girls entered the room. Then the doors shut and the silence grew infinitely larger. Elaine's neighbor drummed her fingers on the tablecloth. Each thump amplified in Elaine's mind, pounding a rhythm in her skull.

What if the dinner was a test? The thought had crossed her mind throughout the day. That she might never make it to the trials, might never have a chance to protect Henry. That she would fail a sibling, again.

The entrance of a tall, finely clothed woman interrupted her thoughts.

"Welcome to Prysnen."

The air seemed to still around the woman. She drifted forward on the dais overlooking the tables, regarding them with an unsettling indifference. Under the glow of the chandeliers, her pale skin looked almost luminescent.

"I trust the accommodations are to your liking." There was something off about the way the woman spoke. Something missing. "Your training will begin tomorrow. You will find your schedules in your room when you return after dinner. Trials will occur every two weeks, as will eliminations. Once the trials conclude, those remaining will be inducted into the Planetary Defense. In exchange for your service, your families will be offered protection. Everything you do counts. Everything you learn matters."

Elaine figured it out, what was wrong with the woman's voice. There was no spark behind her words. They left her lips lifeless and fell flat. She reminded Elaine of a ghost, with her empty words and colorless skin.

"You understand the stakes," she said. *Stakes, stakes, stakes.* That word had become a mantra in and of itself recently. Yes, they understood the stakes—the entire world did—but the ghost-woman repeated them anyway. "You have all been brought here for a purpose. To defend, to protect. To fight. And fight you must. The Fall cannot win, or else humanity is doomed." Perhaps for the first time, emotion slipped through the cracks of her aloof demeanor, but instead of comforting Elaine, the ghost-woman's dread reminded her to be afraid.

The Fall were man-eating martians, said the conspirators. The Fall were an extraterrestrial threat, said the government. The Fall were more advanced than they could ever imagine, said the scientists.

And the Fall were coming.

Then, like a ghost, the woman disappeared as suddenly as she had arrived.

CHAPTER 4

7:00 AM *// Training // Yard*

Elaine checked over the lines of her schedule for what felt like the hundredth time. Training... yard... Mind muddy from a poor night of sleep, she slipped into leggings and a t-shirt and tied her hair into a ponytail. Training before breakfast; her stomach grumbled in protest, but at least she wouldn't heave when she exercised for the first time in a year.

Competitors gathered on the lawn, milling about and looking around like a hive of bees without their queen. Birds chirped in the forest and a frosty morning breeze wound through the cluster of bodies. Elaine scanned the crowd for a familiar face. When she finally noticed Kate standing alone, a booming voice cut through the confusion.

"One lap around the yard!" a man called from the door he stepped out of.

Without hesitation, they began to run. No one knew exactly how eliminations worked, what counted or what didn't. Perhaps they would be dismissed simply for being too slow.

Elaine fought to stay in the middle of the pack, even as each step set her muscles on fire and her abdomen split apart. Her heart thudded against her ribs, begging her to stop and relieve the ache.

They trailed the edge of the lawn where the forest encroached. Elaine barely registered that she passed the path she'd taken the night before because of the sheer amount of concentration it took to force her feet to move. By the end of the lap, her legs quivered, sweat shone on her skin, and her lungs gulped down oxygen greedily. Her face flushed not only from exertion—she'd finished near the back of the group. She shouldn't have expected more, not when she quit dancing a year ago and hadn't worked out since, but still... This was a far cry from who she imagined herself being. Strong, agile. Not this— weak, lethargic.

But she had time. Two weeks until the first trial. She would train to be strong when it counted.

The coach had them form pairs. Elaine ended up with a girl standing nearby who was even taller than she was. The girl had high cheekbones and a strong jawline. Everything about her, from the uptilt of her catlike eyes to the focused line of her mouth, was sharp. "I'm Ava," the girl said while they waited for instructions. The greeting didn't come with a smile.

"Elaine," she replied.

The coach, an imposing figure who looked much older up close, handed Elaine a pair of punching pads that fit like gloves, and drew a line between them with chalk. Elaine slipped the pads on, the adrenaline that had worn off from the run roaring to life again.

"Don't lose your footing," the man said, and as soon as he blew his whistle Ava sprung forward.

At first, Elaine wasn't sure how to react. Ava was strong, and each punch pushed her away from the white line. The punches rained in quick succession, one after the other, until Elaine could feel the garden wall looming behind her.

An expression of victory crossed Ava's face, sending a wave of fury through Elaine.

Elaine readjusted her feet and leaned forward. Each time Ava paused to breathe, Elaine stepped forward. Ava noticed the movement and scowled, redoubling her efforts. But she was only human, and her hits grew weaker and her breathing heavier.

Elaine hid her smile when the whistle blew and the tarnished pigment was beneath her shoes.

"Your turn," Ava huffed, taking the pads from Elaine.

Elaine raised her hands, steadying her breath before the next whistle pierced the air. She launched at Ava and threw her fist at the pad. Pain burst through her hand, the material less forgiving than it appeared. Elaine ignored the sensation and continued striking Ava's outstretched hands.

But Ava had learned from Elaine. For every second Elaine took to catch her breath, Ava forced her back. By the end of the exercise, the line stood behind Ava, taunting Elaine with its intactness. *You didn't put up much of a fight,* the paint seemed to be saying.

After that, the trainer shouted at them to drop to the ground and do various exercises: sit-ups, push-ups, and planks. Then they sprinted another lap, did jumping jacks until Elaine saw stars, and threw a weighted ball heavier than Elaine's upper body. And to finish it all off, they ran another lap dragging a box behind them.

Elaine dry-heaved into the grass once everyone had left. She fell to her knees and stared at her hands, panting.

The hairs on the back of her neck raised. She turned around but never found the source of her unease. From the highest level of the castle, the ghost-woman peered down at her; sunlight glinted off the window and shielded the castle's warden from view.

———

The morning runs gradually became bearable. On a good day, Elaine kept near the front and thought about how nice the breeze felt on her exposed skin. She stopped throwing up on the fourth day.

By the second week, she almost began to look forward to training; she enjoyed the physical strain, the idea that she could run faster, lift heavier, and jump higher.

That was, until the trainer, who they came to learn was named Tom, introduced sparring. It made little sense, shoving them into a patch of grass outlined by chalk and asking them to fight. No battle against the Fall would call for fists—at least, Elaine hoped none would.

Ava and Max went first. They stood in the circle staring at each other, sizing one another up until Tom blew the whistle. Elaine flinched and covered her ears, inching away from Tom so that he wouldn't burst her eardrums.

Max seemed the clear winner. He stood over six feet tall and had the body of an athlete. Football, if Elaine had to guess. He was brawny but quick on his feet, too, dodging Ava's attacks easily.

Once the first minute passed, some began betting, and most of the bets Elaine overheard favored Max.

"Max is gonna win," Mason whispered to her after making sure Tom wasn't looking their way. While their trainer had never explicitly banned talking during the matches, no one wanted to test his lenience.

"I think Ava's going to," Elaine said.

"No way. She hasn't landed a single blow." He gestured to Max spinning around Ava's fists.

Despite her futile attempts to attack Max, Ava didn't seem deterred. If anything, she looked a little smug. Elaine could see why: Ava never meant to pin Max as the spars required. Instead, she planned to edge him out of the circle. Ava had started the spar offensively to put Max on the defense so that he wouldn't pin her first. After that, it was only a matter of deftly edging him back with calculated movements so that he thought he was winning and wouldn't notice the line drawing closer.

"See where they're standing?" Elaine said. Mason followed her gaze. "She's about to win. Look."

It took Mason a moment to see it, but he nodded once he noticed Max's foot shifting outside of the ring. "You were right," he said, in awe as Max finally crossed the line.

Tom's whistle announced the end of the match. Max glanced at the trainer, trying to figure out why the round was over.

"Look down!" someone shouted.

Max glanced down at his feet, catching sight of the smudged chalk, then up at Ava, a dumbfounded expression on his face.

After that first match, no one accidentally stepped outside the ring again.

The next match featured Miranda, whom Elaine recognized as the one who'd asked if they would be killing each other, and a lanky boy with a nervous face. Despite Miranda's many saccharine smiles and attempts to bat her eyes at him, the boy won, leaving the ring without so much as a glance in her direction.

"Elaine Carter! Tether... Nic-oh-les-coo," Tom called out, no doubt mispronouncing her opponent's name.

She blanched at the sound of her name. She had managed to convince herself that she wouldn't spar today. She wasn't ready. She hadn't practiced any moves or devised some brilliant plan to compensate for her lack of fighting experience.

She barely had a moment to steady herself before she was standing in front of her opponent. Her heart sped into overdrive as dozens of razor-sharp eyes focused on her.

Elaine stifled the choke that rose in her throat when she saw her opponent: Tether, the boy from the landing that first day, whose gaze was somehow more disarming now. He stared at her with those cold eyes, and she could *feel* him looking her up and down. He watched her the way a predator appraised its prey, calculating and emotionless.

She studied him, too, and she didn't like her odds. If she had thought the pairing would be fair, that the trainer would at least try to match her with someone her size, she was sorely mistaken. Even with her height, Tether stood a head taller. And his muscles... he wasn't a bodybuilder by any means, but the power in his arms was unmistakable. She could practically hear the bets being placed against her. She didn't stand a chance.

Tether caught her staring, the ghost of a sneer curving his lips. She quickly averted her gaze, the blades of grass suddenly the most interesting thing in the world.

Tom held his hands in the air.

As a dancer, Elaine's strength had never been forcefulness. Balance, endurance, grace—those were what she earned from hours of sweat in the studio. Qualities that honed her into a skilled performer, not a weapon. Certainly not someone capable of wrestling a person twice her size.

The trainer brought his hand down and the whistle screeched.

Elaine flinched, expecting Tether to jump at her. He could take her down easily—she knew it, he knew it. Everyone watching knew it. But he didn't. He simply took a step to the right. Then another, and another.

He was circling her. Elaine would have laughed if she weren't so afraid. She mirrored his movements, staying as far away from him as possible. His step to the right, hers to the left. They moved like that for a few minutes, the only aggression the glint in their eyes. Elaine could feel Tom getting annoyed behind her. The thought distracted her, and she almost missed Tether's muscles going taut.

Why engage in this dance? Why not attack her as soon as the whistle blew? Because Tether wanted her relaxed. He wanted to coax her reflexes into lethargy so that when he did reach for her, she couldn't escape. He'd seen agility in her stance, jumpiness in her fingers twitching at her sides. So he'd eased her into a dance, false comfort in the pattern, in the predictability of it all—lured her then attacked, like a true predator.

Elaine realized all this in the split second before he sprang forward, arms outstretched to wrap around her waist and force her down. He was fast, but she was faster. Twirling out of the way, Elaine watched Tether stumble. When he regained his balance, there was no anger in his expression. But his steadfast resolve scared her more.

Now that the circle had been broken, Tether's movements became unpredictable. He feigned an attack. Then feigned again. Then he actually went for her, again reaching for her torso.

She could have jumped out of the way, again, but Elaine knew that eventually, he would succeed. Eventually, she wouldn't be fast enough; he would get lucky, and she would lose. So instead of evading him, Elaine ducked down and swept his unbalanced legs out from under him.

The thud of his back slamming into the ground made Elaine wince. Unfortunately, her pity was short-lived.

Tether's hand latched onto the bottom of her shirt and he pulled her down with him. She landed on his chest, elbows digging into his ribs.

"5... 4," the trainer began.

Tether smiled boyishly, as though he weren't losing. He had a nice smile, Elaine mused, then banished the thought.

"2..."

In the last second, Tether whispered, "Next time, Carter," and hugged her to him, flipping their bodies so she was the one on the ground. Elaine gritted her teeth against the impact.

"5..." Tom started again. Elaine swore the number carried a hint of amusement.

No matter how much Elaine struggled, Tether's grip on her wrists was unrelenting. She tried kicking and kneeing him, to no avail. She even considered head-butting him, but decided a concussion wasn't worth one spar, not when the trials loomed more important.

"1. Stop!"

The pressure on her wrists released.

Next time, Carter. Elaine glared as he stood.

She wanted to scream. To point out how unfair the fight was, how Tether had every advantage and she had none. But this wasn't about fairness—the Fall likely had every advantage, too.

It was about proving themselves, and Elaine had failed.

CHAPTER 5

There was no training on the Friday of the second week. No classes, either. The castle brimmed with anticipation for the first trial. Servants rushed to prepare breakfast an hour earlier than usual, and competitors glanced over their shoulders as though the trial might creep up on them unannounced. They had fallen into routine—today reminded them that their presence here was not permanent, their survival not a sure thing. Breakfast was quiet.

No one could predict what the trial might be. Those who tried wound up spinning ridiculous tales of gladiator arenas and lion dens.

The ghost-woman beckoned them up a staircase on the far side of the castle, the only one that reached the fifth floor. They followed her, filing through a thin hallway into a large room. Elaine paused at the doorway.

Glossy oak planks crisscrossed the floor, just asking to be waltzed across. Grand chandeliers glittered overhead, jewels begging to be admired as one spun below. Mirrors fit for a giant lined one wall, imploring dancers to appreciate their own beauty.

A ballroom.

For a moment, Elaine thought their trial might be dancing. Then she realized how silly that sounded—fending off starving lions was more likely. Who cared how well they could pirouette?

A thud as one servant shut the heavy door. Two others went around handing out strips of black fabric. *Blindfolds*, Elaine realized once one was in her hand.

"Sit down and cover your eyes," the ghost-woman instructed.

The floor was cool beneath Elaine's palms as she lowered herself to a seated position. Feathery fingers tested her blindfold. Her knot held, and the pressure disappeared.

A minute ticked by in silence. Maybe two. The ghost-woman didn't wish them luck or give any sort of warning for what happened next.

The strangest sensation passed over Elaine, prickling like a million ants climbing over her skin, a roaring in her ears, and her body went numb. Then—

She was floating. Her body was weightless as a wisp of air, surrounded by darkness. It was what she imagined drifting in outer space felt like, except without stars or any sort of scenery. It was

empty.

Peaceful.

Elaine lost track of time, though perhaps she'd never had it in the first place. She wouldn't know—she couldn't think properly. Her mind struggled to form thoughts, and the ones it did were nebulous and nonsensical.

And for whatever reason, she liked it that way.

At some point, a pinprick of light broke through the black fog. A *fog*. Gray wisps of air were all around her, murky and unending. How had she not noticed it before? The gears of her mind began to turn as though freshly oiled. And the light grew brighter; it became the sun above her head.

Up, Elaine thought. The sun was up.

Down... nothing was down. Only inky shadows. But as soon as the thought had formed, the ground rushed up to meet her. The muddy grassland beneath her feet was down.

Gone was the sense of weightlessness; now gravity pulled at her, a steady tug tethering her to the dewy blades of grass.

Feeling returned to her in waves, connecting her conscience to her limbs. Her arms, first, an electric buzz running from her shoulders to the tips of her fingers. Then her legs. Sensation spread to every inch of her body until she became whole again.

Slowly, as though she didn't want to, Elaine realized where she was. The grass, the house in the distance, she recognized them. And the fog—she knew not only where she was, but *when*.

July 21st. The day Lily had died.

The day Elaine had killed her sister.

"Don't go far," Evan had said. Elaine could picture their father seven years ago, letting them run off with that easy smile that used to light up his face. He never smiled like that anymore. Having a child die young did things to a person.

It was Elaine's fault he didn't smile. It was Elaine's fault Helen had acted like a corpse for the past seven years, unable to feel.

Don't go far... If only she had listened. If only she hadn't been so arrogant. Maybe then Lily would still be alive.

But Elaine had always had a sense for where Lily was, in the same way she could *feel* people. Everyone she'd ever met had a sort of hum about them, a beat like the pulse of an artery. Lily most of all.

And because they could find each other so quickly, hide-and-seek was only fun when they went into the woods connected to their backyard. When they went outside that warm summer day, Elaine didn't think twice about the fog rolling in.

Elaine turned her head. Lily was standing next to her. Her dirty blonde hair, the frizzy strands pulled into a loose braid, her brown eyes that glittered gold under sunlight... This was Lily, exactly the way Elaine had obsessed over her for the past seven years.

A part of Elaine yearned to reach for her sister. To hug her and kiss her and cry and scream. But the other part of her, the one in control of her body, was as much an extension of this memory as Lily was.

"Go as far as you want," Elaine told her sister conspiratorially. "You know I'll find you."

Lily only laughed, the sound like a chime in the wind. Elaine missed that laugh. But then again, since Lily's death, she missed a lot of things. "Five-minute head start," she made Elaine promise before running off, her bright blue dress vanishing between the trees.

Most times, Elaine didn't bother waiting all five minutes, but that day she did, daydreaming about something stupid as Lily ran to her death.

Don't go far... go as far as you want. Voices swam in her head—memories. Memories that had haunted her for seven years, attacking her in waves of grief and guilt, but never like this. Never so potently.

Go as far as you want, as far as you want, as far as you want. Elaine's own words became a chant in her mind. An ache that consumed her. A pound that punished her. A pain that condemned her.

No matter how hard Elaine tried to wake up, to silence the voices, she couldn't escape. That detached part of her... deep in her bones, she knew she deserved this. Because she could still remember the moment she couldn't feel Lily anymore. She remembered it so vividly, it became a thing of nightmares.

The fog penetrated the forest at the same time Elaine entered. Its viscous fingers reached for her while she searched. And the air—Elaine specifically recalled how it shifted in the way it always did before it rained in summer.

Even when the first ten minutes passed, Elaine wasn't worried; she could still perceive Lily's presence. It was the thrum in her veins, the buzz on her skin: constant and dependable. Until

it wasn't.

Until that moment Elaine tripped on the root of some scraggly tree and felt a sharp pang. The rush of adrenaline. And then nothing where Lily once was. A gaping emptiness where she once sensed her sister's closeness keenly. Whatever force had connected Elaine to her sister had been snuffed out by an invisible hand.

One moment it was there—Lily was alive—and the next it was gone—Lily was dead.

Elaine stayed in the forest searching for hours, tears of desperation running down her face. Her eyes were red and her pants and arms were covered in dirt and scratches when Helen found her.

"I can't find her," Elaine had said—wailed. "I can't..." And she broke down into sobs. *I can't feel her.* But that didn't mean anything to Helen. It didn't mean anything at all anymore.

Elaine couldn't separate herself from the memory. Everything was too real. The tears staining her cheeks, Helen screaming when they found Lily's body two days later.

Lily already had a tomb when they found her, encased inside a hollow log, her hiding place.

A stupid log.

They never discovered what had killed her. As far as anybody knew, Lily shouldn't have died. Her skin had no marks, and none of the tests they'd ordered detected anything out of the ordinary.

But finding the body wasn't the worst part. Looking into Lily's far-off eyes before Helen gently closed them didn't haunt Elaine as much as that wretched, *happy* feeling that had hit her when the connection went dark.

She'd been *happy.* When she inexplicably felt her sister take her last breath, Elaine had been happy. Euphoric, even.

They'd bickered often growing up, more so than other children their age. And the fights had gotten worse and more explosive with each passing year. But Elaine knew she loved her sister and that Lily had loved her, too. She never doubted that. Except...

Except what if she'd wanted Lily to die? There was no other explanation for the high that rushed through her when Lily's life force went cold. It hadn't faded right away, either. The bliss had stuck with Elaine for the next few weeks, like a sickness she couldn't recover from.

She still felt it sometimes, that peace, like she'd been freed from something evil. But she shoved the feeling to the darkest depths of her soul and tried to forget where it came from, what it meant.

Images flashed before her: the accusation in Helen's eyes, even though she would never speak it, Lily's empty gaze, that stupid log in that stupid clearing. She was no longer trapped in a memory. She was trapped in her own guilt.

Go as far as you want, go as far as you want...

I can't find her, I can't find her... I can't...

Voices swirled in her head, a thunderous storm of guilt. They grew louder, heavier, crueler. And it was her voice that haunted her the loudest.

Go as far as you want!

I can't find her!

I don't want to find her!

I'm happy she's dead! Happy! Elaine's own voice screeched at her, full of hate. *Why are you happy?*

You wanted her to die.

There it was. Most days she was certain she hadn't wished for Lily's death. Today wasn't one of them.

The words consumed her. They were a loathing song that stunted her thinking. She lost herself to the cacophony.

But there were glimpses of who she was—more importantly, why she was here, in this hell of her own making. *Henry.* *The trials.* She had to get back. This was a test. She had to get out. She wouldn't let her sibling die, not again. Not after so freshly reliving Lily's death.

So she reached. She didn't have a body, much less arms, to reach with, but she used her mind. Grasped for anything that might pull her out.

Eventually, she found it. The memory of holding Henry for the first time, a helpless baby born to a doomed world. He stared up at her, his big, blue eyes full of light. She fought for him.

And if she passed the trials, she would fight for everybody.

CHAPTER 6

Elaine regained consciousness slowly—at least she thought she did. Time had no bearing here, deep in the crevices of her mind. She could feel herself returning to her body. She was close. All she had to do was open her eyes—

Something yanked at her from her subconscious. It wrapped its formless fingers around her and dragged her back to that place, that darkness where she had no weight, no form.

And then it spoke to her.

Hello. A rasp like claws grinding against marble. Fear rolled through Elaine, amplified by the emptiness and by the fact that she had no body to absorb it.

This wasn't part of the test. Elaine had stopped the memory. She'd escaped. She'd passed.

She fought against whatever force held her captive, but it was too strong. This was its domain, she realized. Her mind belonged more to this invisible creature than it did to her.

So *desperate to return*, it noted. And it laughed at her struggle, a scratchy cackle. *All in good time. But first, who are you?*

Then it reached for her memories. Elaine couldn't understand how she knew that was what it was doing—she could just *feel* it. It felt wrong, how the creature rummaged through her childhood. And somehow she could sense when it saw Lily.

A *sister*, it said, pausing for a beat. Then it resumed its hunt. But suddenly it stopped again, before it could reach the scene of Lily's death.

Elaine felt something else join them.

It seems I must go, said that terrible voice. *Until we meet again.* Its claws retracted from the painful iron grip it had held her in, and its presence disappeared from her mind.

Then the incomer—whatever had scared off that voice—pulled Elaine back into her body.

When she awoke and peeled off her blindfold, she found the ghost-woman staring at her with an emotion she couldn't place. *Fear?* It flickered and vanished before Elaine could be sure.

CHAPTER 7

"What *was* that?" Elaine remembered Kate asking, fear and awe woven into the question. Elaine didn't know. None of them did. It was something beyond them, whatever had infiltrated their thoughts. Something impossible to understand.

The first trial had sought out the most horrible, guilt-ridden memory it could find. Replayed it and made them relive the nightmare until their hearts were sore and they let go.

That was the point, wasn't it? To drag the guilt out of them and flay them with it until they realized they must abandon the regret, the anger. For the war against the Fall would result in loss. The kind of loss that fractured a person into so many pieces they became unrecognizable. The first trial weeded out those who broke too easily.

Half of their group disappeared that night. No one saw them leave. They were just gone when the sun rose—their rooms empty, their bodies missing from the herd during the morning run.

Eerie. And somehow, the forest looked guilty. The trees swayed almost happily. The dirt appeared darker, as though stained by blood. In the shadows, a silhouette... Elaine blinked. The figure disappeared.

Great, she thought bitterly. Now her mind was playing tricks on her in the daylight, too, fed by the rumors.

How did seventy-five kids disappear without a trace? *They were probably killed. There's probably a graveyard in the forest*, a conspiratorial voice whispered to her, repeating what a gangly boy had said earlier while they waited on the field for Tom to appear.

"You seem tired." For a second, Elaine thought she'd imagined Mason's voice.

"Couldn't sleep," Elaine admitted, focusing on Mason. He wore an easy smile as they waited for names to be called into the ring.

Couldn't sleep was the half of it. *I thought that if I slept that voice would come back and torture me* was the other half she didn't care to share. The half that she worried that an evil spirit was haunting her, that it wanted something from her. That, since the trial, she hadn't been able to stop hearing its rasp echoing in her head.

That confession would have her eliminated faster than she could blink. Perhaps leave her dead. She kept her mouth shut.

"Yeah, I—" Mason started, but was interrupted by his name being called for the first spar. "Wish me luck."

Elaine hated watching the spars. She cringed at the unnecessary pain. Every other match, someone would end up so badly beaten up that they had to visit the nurse before class. Nose crooked, drooling blood at the mouth, knee bent in—Elaine thought she had seen it all, yet there was always a new injury to add to the roster. And somehow, no matter how disfigured, the nurse always made her patients look brand new.

Thankfully, Elaine had never walked away with more than a bruise, and those were usually her own doing.

"Good luck," she said as Mason turned to the ring.

A *friend...* Elaine mused, but locked the idea away. Friends couldn't exist in a zero-sum game. Not one with lives hanging in the balance.

Mason appeared calm as he stepped over the white line, as he always did, calmer than anyone ever looked before their round. His opponent, an equally well-built redhead whom Elaine saw around Tether often, almost matched his confidence.

At the whistle's cry, the redhead—those betting called him Jace—threw himself at Mason, aiming a fist at his stomach. Instead of twisting away, Mason *let* Jace hit him. And barely flinched when the punch landed. Then he grabbed Jace's freckled forearm and yanked him to the ground.

Agony flashed in Jace's eyes as he fell. By the small choke he gave, Elaine imagined Mason had pulled hard enough to sprain Jace's arm. *Thump*—Jace hit the ground. Elaine was close enough to hear him wince. Close enough to see the look on Mason's face as he pinned his opponent down. Empty.

Mason's eyes were empty, even when the trainer held up his stopwatch and exclaimed, "46 seconds, a new record!" His gaze was glassy, as though he were somewhere else. Distant. Not happy for winning so quickly, not angry at Jace for the bruise on his abdomen. He just stood there quietly until Jace got up, exiting the circle without so much as a flicker of emotion crossing his face.

"Nice job," Elaine said stupidly, regretting the words as soon as Mason looked at her.

He paused like he was just noticing she was there. "Thanks."

By the end of the next match, Mason looked more like himself. "Do you believe what they're saying about them killing us?"

No, she didn't. Judging by Mason's untroubled expression, Elaine doubted he did, either. "Not really. Why would they?"

Mason shrugged. "People might riot if they knew our families get access to the National Bunker," he suggested.

Elaine frowned. She hadn't thought about it that way. "But then wouldn't they have to kill our families, too?"

"I guess so. But maybe the ones that pass the trials, their families wouldn't say anything so they can keep their spot. But the ones who are eliminated have nothing to lose by running their mouth." He paused, the weight of his statement sinking in: winning didn't guarantee survival, but losing would be a swift execution before the Fall even arrived.

Words jumbled in Elaine's head. How did one respond to that? "All the more reason to pass," she finally settled on, but her voice shook.

"Hey," Mason implored her to look at him. "We will." The finality in those two words did little to ease the tight yoke of anxiety.

Henry, I'm trying, she wanted to tell him.

"Besides, they're just rumors."

No one has found the bodies yet, Elaine translated silently. Because she had stayed awake all night with an unobstructed view of the driveway, and only one car had passed through the iron gates.

A single car with a single passenger, a man who had entered the castle in the dead of night, the sound of his arrival masked by the symphony of chirping crickets. Who the man was, Elaine could only guess. All she knew was that he was not the seventy-five missing competitors.

At dinner that night, attached to the far wall below the high windows, was a list of names—their names. Thick black lines had been slashed across the bottom half of the list.

They reminded Elaine of blades slitting skin.

CHAPTER 8

Lack of sleep did three things to a person. One: headaches. Splitting ones that made you want to crawl out of your skin. Two: torpor. Muscles that refused to move, as though your entire body were filled with sand. Three: irritability. Every inconvenience, no matter how minute, let loose a storm of anger that far exceeded the situation.

Elaine experienced all three keenly. Her skull pounded like her brain had switched places with her heart. All she could hear was the blood pumping in her ears. Her shoulders slumped forward. Invisible weights were attached to her feet. The lawn seemed bigger, suddenly, the lap stretching on forever, and longer still. She raged internally at Tom barking orders.

"You look terrible," Kate commented at the end of training.

And, with Elaine, a lack of sleep tended to bring back her ghosts.

The words gave Elaine pause. *You look terrible*, she heard them clearly, but not in Kate's butterfly voice. Lily giggled them inside her head instead.

Guilt was like the tides. Waning, but never fully gone. The moisture of a million tears left in its wake. And returning with the force of a crashing wave when one least expected it to.

Elaine blinked. Saw Lily standing there, not Kate. Her vision shifted between the two. Lily—Kate—Lily—confused blue eyes—innocent brown ones—a face flushed from Tom's exercises—one pale from being dead, so very dead...

"Elaine? I didn't mean it. You just look a little tired is all. It's not that bad," Kate said, rushing to amend her statement.

"No, you're right. I look terrible." Midnight swirled around her puffy eyes and her hair was stuck in a day-old bun. Elaine tried to laugh, but it sounded forced. "I haven't been able to sleep."

"Why?"

"Not sure. Anxiety, I guess."

Kate nodded like she understood, but she didn't—couldn't possibly—understand what kept Elaine from sleeping. Slipping away into a dreamland terrified her. Falling into a trance, into a place where that *voice* could find her... speak to her... ransack her memories like it owned them...

And the worst part of it all was that she swore she could feel it trying to slither into her head once the sun set. Ghost claws pressing on her skull. Phantom whispers of that horrid rasp filling her ear. Elaine's shiver had nothing to do with the autumn wind.

After training, they all crossed the lawn, sprinting upstairs to get ready in the short time allotted before the first class began at nine. She felt dirty, like an invisible grime coated every inch of her body. She darted into the communal showers on the third floor, making a beeline for the only empty cubicle. Someone grumbled behind her as she pulled the curtain across. In the six minutes it took to wash her hair and scrub the feeling of filth from her skin, the line had grown into the hall.

She chanted the pillars of Sun Tzu's *The Art of War* in her head as she headed to her room.

Victorious warriors win first then go to war, while defeated warriors go to war first and then seek to win.

If you know yourself but not the enemy, for every victory gained you will suffer a defeat.

One mark of a great soldier is that he fights on his own terms or fights not at all.

Foreknowledge must be obtained from people, people who know the conditions of the enemy.

She tended to linger on those which seemed to doom humanity, though she had memorized them all in preparation for today. She revised her notes at the windowsill before packing everything away, slinging her bag over her shoulders and taking the stairwell down to the ground floor.

The circular tower that housed the stairs let out into a large drawing room furnished with plush velvet sofas and armchairs facing a vacant marble hearth. Resting atop the mantel was the portrait of a woman whose twinkling eyes betrayed the facade of gravity. The hint of a smile curved her crimson lips, an expression the artist had taken great care to capture. Elaine thought it fitting that the only painting that featured a smile hung in the most central room.

She spared the woman a glance as she passed through the drawing room and into a long hall that turned into another long hall that led into a shorter hall where Kron held Strategies of War. A stone from the garden propped open the door to the classroom.

Four others had already claimed their desks in the first row. It had become a sort of competition in Kron's class to show up the earliest. His favorites changed depending on who was the most punctual and who gave the smartest answers. And if someone clambered into class even a minute late, he would pelt them with questions until he found a subject they hadn't mastered, then tailor their exam to trip them up. Once the first victim had suffered—falling a whole rank by the end of class—all of Kron's students arrived many minutes early.

Elaine lay her bag against the legs of her chair and rehearsed *The Art of War* a final time. Once the desks filled, Kron removed the door stopper, setting the rock on the edge of his desk, and went to the front of the room. "You have an hour," he said, then handed the first desk of each column a stack of papers.

He motioned for them to begin after the exams reached the last row. Like the stirrings of leaves in a haunted forest, they flipped open the first sheet of paper.

We have discussed in class the famous tale of the concubines to put into perspective Sun Tzu's teachings. In what ways is this lesson still applicable today? How would you apply the tale's lesson?

Elaine recalled the story of a general tasked with training the emperor's concubines, only to find the women uncooperative. They would laugh at the general's instructions and execute the drills poorly. To enforce order, the general had ordered the emperor's favorite beheaded. The concubines executed the drills flawlessly after that, becoming perfect soldiers. Or so the story went.

Although Sun Tzu hadn't spun that particular tale (many texts speculated his followers had), the story of the concubine army drew from the master's writing. It reflected his leadership principles: maintain discipline and act decisively.

Elaine began writing. *The lesson of using fear to enforce order is still applicable today. However, one nuance that arises is multiple sources of fear. Need a general instill fear in soldiers already afraid of their enemy? I would argue that a general should not give his soldiers yet another reason to be afraid by threatening their lives if they are already fearful. Instead, I would use their existing fear of the enemy to encourage discipline and preciseness.*

As she set her pencil down and rolled her wrist to relieve the muscles cramping in her hand, Elaine mused briefly about the disappearances. Whoever oversaw the trials believed in compounding fear; they added to the fear of the Fall with a fear of being killed for failing. The uncertainty and rumors surrounding the vanishings further exacerbated their fear.

She breezed through the rest of the exam. Until the final question. She paused, staring at it, willing the words to make sense. *What did Sun Tzu mean by: "A good general knows to send the elderly before the young, and the young before the seasoned soldiers. A bad general wastes his best in the front lines without tiring his enemy first."*

The question itself didn't bother Elaine so much as the nagging familiarity of the quote. In fact, it might have been the simplest query of the exam; all she had to do was translate Sun Tzu into her own words and apply it to a historical battle. Yet the quote, the way she felt like she had seen it before but also couldn't remember its place in the text, perturbed her.

She had poured over Sun Tzu's work. She had read *The Art of War* from front to back, back to front, then front to back all over again. She had committed to memory every one of his sayings, shoving his words into her brain no matter how little sense they made or how they all seemed to blend together near the end. She had read every interpretation of Sun Tzu she could get her hands on. And she had tested herself a dozen times, hammered her mistakes onto the page until they withered into nothing. Until she was perfect.

So why, after everything, could she not recall this one?

She squeezed her eyes shut in frustration and forced herself to stay calm. The last thing she needed was to panic. But when her gaze drifted up to the clock, a fresh wave of alarm hit her. Four minutes left.

Just start writing, you idiot, she chided herself. All she had to do was phrase the quote in her own words and apply it to a historical battle. The Battle of Crécy would work. There—done. And yet...

Elaine realized what held her from putting pen to paper. Sun Tzu had never written that. The question's quote was a *misinterpretation* of the great Chinese thinker's writing. She glared at the ruse of a question and scribbled her answer.

Kron cleared his throat. Pens clattered nervously onto desks. They passed the booklets to the front of the room, where Kron stood to collect them.

"Mason," Kron called, and Mason's head snapped to attention. "If you had many tributary states, and were warring against an empire stronger than yourself, what would you do?"

"Throw the people of my tributary states at the enemy until they're weakened enough for me to fight them."

Kron moved on, and Mason looked relieved. "Miranda, what did Sun Tzu mean by: 'A good general knows to send the elderly before the young, and the young before the seasoned soldiers; a bad general wastes his best in the front lines without tiring his enemy first?'"

In that shrill voice of hers that made Elaine want to claw at her ears, Miranda said, "He meant that you should put the inexperienced soldiers at the front lines to wear out your enemy's best fighters. That way, once they're tired, you strike with your best soldiers. An example of this can be found in the Battle of Ts—"

"Incorrect. Sun Tzu never wrote that. Which you would know if you studied properly."

Miranda ground her teeth as the entire class seemed to deflate in disappointment. Other than Elaine, only Ava and Tether appeared to have answered the question correctly.

"Elaine," Kron said, and she focused her gaze on the decorated ex-general. He was a burly man with graying hair and a wide grin that lit his face when he discussed the historical tales of great battle strategy. "Do you agree with the idea of throwing the elderly, and next the youth at the enemy before the true soldiers?" He had a way of speaking that made it sound like he had no opinion, even though Elaine felt sure he did.

She gave the prompt thought before saying, "It depends. If you sacrifice everyone but the soldiers, there will be no one to provide for the army. But at the same time, if that battle could win the war, it would be worth it."

Miranda raised her hand. "I disagree. It's wrong to sacrifice people just because they're inexperienced."

"Wrong?" Mason scoffed. "It's war. Everything's wrong. The only thing that's not wrong is winning."

"It's not a matter of wrong or right," Ava said, tapping a finger on her desk thoughtfully. "But if you sacrifice the young, even if you win, what future does the country have? You can't throw away the future for the chance of winning."

"Then why are we here?" Tether asked. To that, no one had a quick response.

Kron studied him. "Ours is not a war like what you'll read in the textbooks, son. Ours is not a war in which we can pretend to understand the enemy. Ours is a war that threatens the entire race. Ours is a war that demands blood and sacrifice, indiscriminate of age. You all are the lucky ones, whether you see it now or not. You will be prepared. You will steel yourselves before battle. You've tricked yourselves into thinking it's your *choice* to fight. But when the Fall finally reach Earth... God save the rest of us."

Kron had years of military experience; he had climbed the ranks from private to a two-star general.

Kron had a passion for histories of brilliant underdogs overcoming terrible odds.

It should have scared them more that he thought they couldn't win.

CHAPTER 9

"Let me just grab it..." Mason's voice trailed as he studied the rankings. "From my room," he finished.

Elaine glanced at the list once more. *Fifteenth.* Fifteen meant safe, for now. Not high enough to stop worrying, though Elaine doubted she could ever stop worrying, even if she were seventh like Mason. Or first like Ava.

She followed Mason to his room, a floor below her own. Unlike her, Mason didn't have a sitting room, just a larger bedroom. Even so, the space felt cramped because of the clutter. Old clothes lay in piles on the floor, waiting to be washed, papers were strewn out in no obvious order over his desk, and his bed lay unmade.

He noticed her staring. "Sorry about the mess."

"It's fine," she said, banishing the stricken look on her face.

He grabbed his bag from underneath his mattress. When he made to leave the room, she asked, "Are we going to the library?"

He shook his head, an excited rush to the motion. "Nah. Follow me."

She hadn't a clue where they were going. Not the main drawing room downstairs, as Mason walked straight past the stairwell. And not the second-floor common room, a circular space enclosed by smooth stone columns separated by walls of glass where other competitors studied.

He finally stopped at the square end of an isolated hallway. It had no doors and seemed to have been constructed for the sole purpose of displaying a woven tapestry of a field of flowers. She doubted anyone had been here for a long while. She doubted the servants had bothered sweeping the carpet here for an even longer while, if they ever had. "I'm not sitting on the floor," she said.

"I know," Mason said with a laugh. Then he pulled aside the tapestry to reveal a dimly lit hallway.

Elaine's breath left her in an impressed gasp. "Where does it go?" she asked as he stepped over the part of the stone wall left over to hide the passage.

"Another library. It's tiny, though."

Elaine didn't conceal her excitement. "Have you read any of the books?" The ghost-woman's words echoed in her head. *Everything you do counts, everything you learn matters.*

Mason shook his head. "I found it yesterday. I didn't have time because I was studying for Kron's test." They neared the end of the hall. Elaine could make out a brighter wash of light ahead.

The passage dropped into a library. Elaine took in the rows of books, the glint of sunlight on the metal muntins of the windows. It reminded Elaine of the quaint bookstore in her hometown. She'd visited the store often with Lily, and while her sister enjoyed perusing the aisles, taking her sweet time to run her eyes over each book that caught her attention, Elaine had always found the place boring.

But this wasn't any old bookstore. This was Prysnen, the host of the trials. This hidden library could hold riddles and clues and all sorts of useful information.

While Mason grabbed his notes, Elaine pulled out the first book that caught her attention, a periwinkle fabric spine wrinkled in the center. She weighed it in her palm. If one could describe a book as fat, this one would merit the title. It wasn't large, per se, not in the way a textbook was. It fit in the palm of her hand, and holding it up didn't take much effort. But the cover couldn't seem to stay shut, too many pages stuffed into too thin a spine, giving the illusion of a bursting belly.

Elaine flipped the book open to the first page, eyes wide with anticipation.

Paper is precious.

She turned over the words in her mind like they were rocks hiding a sparkling treasure. Perhaps the alliteration of the "p" sound meant something?

She flipped to the next page.

Paper is precious.

Then she thumbed through the entire book.

Paper is precious... Paper is precious... Paper is precious... Paper is... precious...

She glared at the pasty parchment. If paper was so *precious*, why waste so much of it on a single, useless sentence?

With aggression, she shoved the book back into place and pulled out the next one, an unmarked sliver of white. She opened the cover and stifled the urge to groan.

Paper is precious.

She combed through the remaining pages and almost threw the book out the window. How many times could a person print such a daft line? Apparently enough times to fill an entire library. By the fifth book Mason joined her search. They went through almost half of the first shelf before finally giving up.

"Come on, we've got better things to do," Mason said, nudging her shoulder when she refused to move.

"But what if one of the books says something different, like a clue about the next trial, and this whole thing was a test to see if you'd go through all the other books to find it?"

He raised his eyebrows at the suggestion. "That would take an entire day."

"So? It would be worth it."

He glanced at his watch. "I'll come back with you tomorrow, if you want, but for now I've got to work on the pre-lab and I'll bet you've got some work to do, too. We've only got another thirty minutes until lunch ends."

She did have work to do. Wren's chemistry assignments never failed to stump her. The particular set she was stuck on wasn't due until Thursday, but if she didn't tackle it now she'd only lose sleep over it later. They fell into a comfortable silence, heads bent over the desk in concentration.

Mason's pencil circled something on the paper. "You know, something's been bugging me about the Games."

The Strategy Games were games in name only; they were easy to mess up and known to mess with ranks. But despite popular opinion, Elaine enjoyed the Games. Strategy was by far her most competent subject.

"The farthest I've gotten to was the mountain pass, but then the ogre kills off my soldiers because I've got barely any left by then," he continued. "I'm pretty sure it's why Gino passed me."

"The ogre's part of the second game, right? The one where you have to destroy the kingdom of Jewn?" Elaine had entered the fifth yesterday. Mason nodded. "Alright. So how many soldiers did you have by the mountain pass?"

He cringed. "Ten."

"Ten?" she balked, then felt bad, so she willed her face into a neutral expression. "How many times have you played it?"

Another wince, and red tinged his tan skin. "Four."

Four? She'd only ever had to cede to a game once, and that was to the first one when she was still learning how the Games functioned. "Okay," she said, twisting in her chair to get a better look at his paper. Between the pages of his pre-lab he'd been scribbling about the Game, but his handwriting was nearly illegible. "Walk me through what you did."

So he recounted his journey.

He had started with an army of two hundred, marched them down the main road to lay siege on the southernmost kingdom for supplies. Along the way he'd lost ten of his men to rogue bandits and another twenty to a sandstorm.

She held her tongue as he went on. Once he'd made it to the southern kingdom, he laid siege on the outer walls with half of his men; the other half hijacked ships to attack the city from behind. He lost a hundred soldiers before he conquered the city and raided the famed armory for better weapons.

Then he'd set sail for the eastern islands, hopping from landmass to landmass on his way to the enemy. He engaged in a skirmish with pirates, and so by the time he reached the ogre, his numbers had whittled to ten.

"Huh," Elaine said. "You realize that every time you had a choice, you chose to fight, right?"

Mason looked confused, so she began to explain what she had done. "First, with the bandits, promise to pay them a lot of gold if they don't attack. Tell them you're on your way to pick up some gold from a mercenary job in the South Kingdom. Then kill them in their sleep before they realize you're lying. When you reach the South Kingdom's capital, don't attack. Wait for the mayor to come out and tell him that you plan on attacking Jewn, and that you'll trade him Jewn's grain stores in exchange for his weapons. You know that Jewn has good agriculture because of all their rivers. If he gives you a hard time, point out how bad the famine is and eventually he'll cave."

"How do you know there's a famine?" Mason asked.

"Oh, sorry, I forgot—you have to first poison the agricultural water so they're starving by the time you get there. The aquifer's on the way, just make sure no one sees you, or else the plan won't work. Do it at night," she said. "And the pirates hate Jewn because Jewn's cracked down on their smuggling, so if you tell them what you're doing they'll join your ranks and you can attack Jewn from the water, too. And for the ogre it's better to just go around the mountain. He's nearly impossible to beat. "The trick is to avoid fighting." Or, as Sun Tzu had put it, *The supreme art of war is to subdue the enemy without fighting.*

Mason stared at his paper, at the decisions which must have suddenly seemed so foolish. "Thank you," he said, looking up.

She shook her head. "No need."

"No, really, Elaine, I mean it," he said. "Thanks."

He thanked her so ardently in part because among the competitors, help was seldomly given. To find someone willing to even share their notes if you missed class was rare—unless they purposely wrote down the incorrect information, which happened frequently. To find someone willing to walk you through their solution to a game was a miracle.

But Mason could be an ally, and now he owed her a favor.

In the words of an ancient Turkish historian Kron had assigned them reading on, *An alliance is only as great as fear of the enemy.* And Elaine feared failing the trials more than anything.

CHAPTER 10

The forest hosted the second trial. Two servants led them across the lawn, September gusts trailing behind. Not a single cloud impaired the crisp blue of the sky. Mud, fresh from last night's rain, squelched under the stampede of human feet. Elaine stared at her boots, more earth than rubber by the time they reached a clearing in the forest.

Granite protruded from the ground in flat slabs. The servants stopped atop the rock and one pulled a slip of parchment from his pocket. Like a town crier reading the king's proclamation, he shouted the contents of the scroll. "The game is capture the flag."

A *game*, Elaine scoffed internally. Funny way of phrasing something with the power to end or save lives.

"In your bags you have a flare gun. One setting shoots a flare, the other immobilizes a member of the opposing team for two minutes. You have one flare and three immobilization shots." Team? Since when did the trials have teams?

At the mention of a gun, Elaine's bag weighed heavier on her shoulders.

"The flare should only be used in emergencies or to burn your opponent's flag. Once you shoot your flare up, you will be escorted off the premises and no longer able to participate in the game." Elaine could practically hear the ghost-woman speaking the instructions in that curt, dull voice of hers. "The goal is simple: capture and burn the other team's flag with a flare. Top two ranks select teams."

Murmurs swept through the clearing as Ava and Jace positioned themselves beside the town crier.

Since she was first rank, Ava chose first. Elaine wondered what it felt like, standing up there, knowing she was better. Safer.

"Elaine," Ava said.

Mason and Kate turned to her inquisitively. Why would Ava choose her first? Twelve other candidates ranked higher, and Elaine didn't think they were friends.

Ava said nothing as Elaine moved to her side.

"Tether," said Jace.

Elaine could feel his stare. Tether gave his friend a conspiratorial grin, then peered at her, his gaze ever probing, ever alluring. She ignored him. *Next time, Carter.* The only words he had ever spoken to her, and for nothing more than to taunt her. To let her know he found her efforts amusing.

It took all of ten minutes to form the teams. They chose either by name or by pointing. The other team called Mason. Ava beckoned Kate with a finger.

The servant who had remained silent gestured to the left and right. "You have fifteen minutes to hide your flag. It must be hidden within one hundred feet of your base, which is already marked, and it must be visible. We will check. The game ends when a flag is burned."

Let the games begin.

"Found it," Ava said.

She marched towards their base, a burned tree with a bright blue "X" painted on its trunk. Like dutiful soldiers, the rest of the team followed. The ashen tree was alone in its misery, black and gnarled in a sea of green and lush. No leaves to nourish. Withered spindles for branches. And defiled with paint, yet another marker of its misfitness.

Ava set her bag against the tree and crouched down, rummaging through it.

"Where's the flag?" someone asked.

"Here," Ava said, standing with a crumpled blue cloth in her hand. "Any ideas where we should hide it?"

A bird chirped in the distance. Leaves rustled in the wind. Water rushed in a nearby stream. No one spoke. Strangely, they looked to Elaine, as though waiting for her to come up with something. Perhaps her expression gave away the flash of an idea.

"There's a river around here. Hear it?" Elaine paused, hoping someone would confirm the sound. Her senses seemed to enjoy betraying her as of late. After a few nods, she continued. "What if we hide it *in* the water? That way, even if they find it, it'll be too wet to burn, and it's still technically visible."

"Giving us more time to find their flag," Ava nodded along. "Alright. Elaine, you're in charge of guarding it."

Ava held the flag out to Elaine. The cloth was surprisingly soft. It shimmered under the rays of light that pierced the canopy, almost iridescent. Submerging it beneath the river felt wrong, its beauty tarnished by dirt and sludge.

"Now what?" Kate asked when Elaine drew her hands from the water.

"Check if you can see it."

Kate drifted to the riverbank and peered over Elaine's shoulder. "Barely."

"Good. Let's go back."

Elaine nodded to Ava upon returning to the base. *The flag is hidden.*

After a short discussion, the seekers were off. Only three remained to defend the flag: Elaine, Kate, and a short boy who sat beside Elaine in their Strategies of War class.

"Let's split up," Elaine said. "Kate, stay here. Quinn, you see that log over there?" He nodded. "Hang around there. I'll stay closer to the river."

Elaine leaned against the trunk of the tree nearest to the water. Its roots extended into the river, shaded with moisture. Bark scratched her skin through her shirt. She focused on the spot where she had buried the flag ten feet away. Minutes slid away with the current. She stared and stared and stared as nothing happened.

Then crashing. Someone cursing. A shout followed by a pained groan—the deep voice sounded familiar.

Elaine signaled to the other two to remain where they were and slipped from her post. The water sloshed against her boots as she trod across the river. Sludge seeped into the gap between rubber and calf. Elaine ignored the discomfort of water and dirt soaking through her socks.

The commotion came from an outcropping of rocks a yard from the river. As Elaine neared, she heard rustling and stunted breathing. Wary of a trap, she led with her gun and glanced over the stone. Behind the slabs of rock was a sharp drop, nearly seven feet deep, and an unmoving body covered in earth. The person lay face-down, but Elaine knew who it was.

"Tether?" she hissed.

After trying and failing to lift his head, he winced and mumbled, "Carter?"

Still hesitant, Elaine called out, "How'd you fall?"

Another unnatural pause. "Tripped." He attempted to turn onto his back, but fell. He grunted in pain. "My shoulder's dislocated. I can't move... but this—this has happened before. I know how to fix... it." He finally shifted his head so that he could see her. His face had taken on a red flush. "I need you... to put it back in."

"How do I know you're not going to immobilize me?" Elaine asked, slowly approaching despite her reservations.

Tether tried to laugh, but it came out as a cough. "My gun is too far... by the time I reach... it, you... you shoot me." He sighed. "Besides, I used the last... restraint."

Elaine paused above the chasm to confirm that more than an arms-length separated Tether and his bag. "Okay—I'm coming. If you reach for your gun, I'm leaving you here."

Her insides churned to witness the sheer amount of pain wracking Tether's body. His arm stuck out crooked. No matter her distaste for him, she couldn't bear to stand by while he suffered. Quickly scanning the forest for any threat to the flag, Elaine climbed down the ledge once she was certain they were alone.

"Deal," Elaine thought she heard Tether mutter, but the rush of air in her ears muffled the sound. The ground flew up to meet her. She bit her lip against the tremor that shot up her leg.

"Are you okay?" Tether asked, gaze shrouded by injury. His concern gave Elaine pause. For a heartbeat, a look of guilt passed over his features, but it vanished instantly.

Tether watched her approach, jaw clenched and eyes tight. In an attempt to smile, he grimaced.

"Is anyone on your team around?" Elaine's knuckles whitened, fingers wrapped tightly around the handle of her gun.

"Came alone... wanted to find flag... alone." He fought a battle to get each word out.

Of course he wanted to be the sole reason his team won—he would receive more points that way. But tripping into a ditch? That was just stupid. Borderline comical.

"You said you know how to fix it?" Elaine prompted, dreading whatever she would have to do. His jacket was unzipped and had fallen off his side, revealing the skin of his left shoulder. A grotesque mass protruded at the edge of his collarbone and a dimple sucked inwards beside it. Elaine suppressed the vomit rising in her throat.

Tether nodded, cheek sweeping over dirt. "Put your knee in my axilla... grab my hand. And pull... straight up...

no matter... no matter how much I... scream, keep pulling. You need to tire out... my shoulder muscles to get it back in," he panted.

She kneeled into his body softly at first. Despite her gentleness, he cried out. Elaine quickly realized she needed to ignore his agony, or else she would never get through it. She needed to do this—Tether needed her to do this. So she gritted her teeth, wrapped her fingers around his wrist, and pulled with all her might. Tether thrashed beneath her and Elaine pressed harder into him to keep him down. After thirty seconds, she couldn't take it anymore, so she averted her gaze to the sky. His limbs contorted. Branches were hurled here and there. Then she heard a hollow clunk and he went limp.

Tether sunk into the ground, his expression peaceful when she finally looked at him.

When Elaine let go of his hand, instead of dropping to his side, it thumped onto his chest.

"Ow." But his smile gave him away before she could feel remorse.

"How about a thank you?" Elaine huffed, standing.

"Thank you, Carter," he said, then blinked at the sky as though suddenly lightheaded. "Could you shoot the flare on my gun? I hit my head pretty hard. I think I might have a concussion. I would do it myself but my hand feels kind of numb..."

Elaine glanced at his gun, then at her own.

He coughed. "Elaine... my gun," he groaned. "Send up my flare." A beseeching pause. "Please." Then his eyes, which had watched her so closely, even through the intensity of her relocating his bone, finally shut—and stayed closed even as she shouted his name.

Perhaps Elaine should have questioned him more—how he had come to fall so terribly, as lithe as he was, how he had managed to wind up just close enough for her to hear. Perhaps she should have paid more attention to what Tether was doing with his right arm instead of staring at the clouds like a coward. Perhaps she should have thought twice before pulling the trigger on Tether's gun.

Perhaps, most of all, she should not even have tried to help.

But Elaine's fault was one of conscience. She refused to allow any more pain to stain her hands, not when she could prevent it. She pulled the trigger, sent a bright burst of light skyward, and dropped down to her knees to sit next to him. "You'll be okay. Help's on the way."

Curiously enough, the ghost-woman emerged from the trees calling Elaine's name, not Tether's. Then he rose. In one fluid motion, he went from unconscious to balancing perfectly on his own. Elaine was still at his feet, too stunned to move.

Tether looked down at her, the fog gone from his eyes. He picked up his gun, the one still lying on the ground. The one Elaine had thought was hers because it was exactly where she'd left it. Except he had switched them while she was distracted fixing his shoulder. Her gaze flitted to the lake in a split second of inanity.

He leered at her mistake. "I would say better luck next time, but I'm not sure there'll be a next time for you."

CHAPTER 11

The entire walk back to the castle, the ghost-woman said nothing.

You failed, whispered that voice in Elaine's head. *Now Henry will die at your hands.* She pushed against it, but no matter how hard she tried not to listen, she couldn't stop herself. Because it was her voice, and it was the truth. And the truth was eating her alive.

She had failed. Failed miserably and completely. She wondered how far her rank would drop. Enough to have her eliminated? Maybe. Probably. Perhaps she would solve the mystery of the vanishing children first-hand.

"Here you are," said the ghost-woman. Without waiting for a reply, she drifted away.

The fire cracked and hissed in its marble cage. It sounded oddly like a cackle. Like if the flames suddenly transformed into a person, that person would be laughing at her. Elaine shook away the thought. Self-pity never saved a dying man.

Everything you do counts, everything you learn matters, rang in her head. As if in answer, her blood rushed to her heart and it pattered violently against her ribs as some suppressed instinct led her to the library.

Elaine had only visited the library a few times when she wanted to study in overwhelming quiet. This time was different. In the emptiness, a quiet hum filled her ears. A buzz danced over her skin.

This feeling, it had been here since she'd first arrived, burrowed somewhere inside her. Prowling silently. And now, alone, the castle empty but for a few servants and the ghost-woman, it roared to life. It felt familiar, in a way, this rush. Elaine couldn't explain it.

When she stood near a specific wall—a specific bookshelf—the sensation flared, becoming achingly acute. In her desperate mind, it was a sign leading her to salvation.

She held a hand out, the tips of her fingers brushing against leather spines. Goosebumps rose along the length of her arm. Elaine paused, studying the book her hand was touching. She pulled it off the shelf and turned it over. *The Snare of Genetics*. Dust from the top of the pages flew into her mouth. She coughed and took a step back. The buzz faded ever so slightly. Elaine frowned. So it wasn't a book that was calling to her... the bookshelf itself was.

Elaine studied the shelves more closely. She paid attention to the grain of the wood, the wear of age on the leather. The dust.

Her eyes widened. Two of the books were missing a layer of dust, as though someone had borrowed them recently. With hesitant excitement, Elaine slid *The Snare of Genetics* back into place and grabbed the dustless books. One fell into the cradle of her hand, but the other only leaned back, fastened to the shelf. Like a lever.

She waited for something to happen. For the bookshelf to rumble and reveal a passageway, but nothing of the sort occurred. The bookshelf didn't so much as quiver.

Elaine glowered at the wood that refused to move. She reached behind the book for the lever's mechanism. Her fingers ran over a switch hidden under the hollow interior of the book. Elaine flipped it open and held her breath.

A faint click, and then—the bookshelf unclasped itself from the wall. Elaine reached into the crease between wood and stone, swinging the secret door open.

Behind was an arched entrance to a hallway drenched in shadows. Elaine swallowed as she stared into its depths. Thick, curling shadows beckoned her forward. For a moment, she was frozen in place. The darkness was direful. It held secrets, the kind that could shatter a heart. But electricity caressed her skin, urging her forward. Inexplicably, Elaine knew whatever was down there was the source of the thrumming in her blood.

Despite her better judgment, Elaine obeyed the whispers of her soul, shifted a foot into the darkness, then succumbed to it completely.

Her eyes were useless here. Dragging one hand along the stone wall, Elaine guided herself by touch instead. She walked in a straight line for several paces. Then the wall curved and the floor dropped. Elaine cried out as she lost her footing. Her ankle twisted as she fell against the wall, hip slamming into stone. A string of curses escaped her mouth as she regained her balance. She rubbed the spot on her arm where a bruise would surely form and wondered if she should turn back.

No. The ferocity of the thought caught Elaine off guard. That strange tug overwhelmed any logic that might warn her away.

Whatever was down here, she needed to see it. It was calling to her.

The stairs wound down cyclically. Elaine kept a hand on the wall for support. Forever passed before she reached the bottom. At least, Elaine felt as though it had. She wouldn't be surprised if she was halfway down the mountain by now.

Her vision had adjusted to the darkness by the time the staircase released her. Elaine gaped at what she had discovered: a cavernous dungeon, its ceiling too far above her head to make out. A sliver of glass let the smallest drip of sunlight in, though the shadows still dominated here. And two rows of cells stretching down for ages.

Somewhere, a rat squeaked. Elaine yelped. *It's just a mouse,* she assured herself.

Stronger than her fear, though, was that energy. That spark of current running through her body, electric and familiar and frightening. It steered her to a cell on the far side of the dungeon.

Her hands trembled as she crossed the darkness. Something was behind those iron bars—or some*one.* Elaine hesitated, the folly of traveling down here finally sinking in. If the bookcase closed, she might be stuck here forever. Or until thirst withered her into nothing. She was deep enough in the earth that no one would hear her screams.

Elaine approached the cell. She could tell it was the right one because her body was on fire. At first, she couldn't see anything. Just the same shadows that had followed her here. Then...

A pair of eyes. Pure obsidian eyes.

Elaine stumbled back, stifling a scream.

The prisoner drifted toward the bars—a young girl. A young girl with midnight black hair that hung to her shoulders, dressed in a muted blue hospital gown in perfect condition. She tilted her head at Elaine as though curious, the motion jerky.

There was something off about the girl's stance, something wrong in the way her eyes glowed with fervor. Something wrong in the way she looked at Elaine: like she wanted to swallow her whole. Like she wanted to tear her into a million unsalvageable pieces.

Without warning, the prisoner shrieked. A loud, piercing cry that echoed in the emptiness, coursing through the shadows. Like a rabid animal, the sound clawed at Elaine's ears, at her mind. Elaine recoiled, trying to cover her ears, but the sound was *in* her. It had infiltrated her brain.

The prisoner's wail reverberated in her bones and filled her head. Elaine couldn't think—she couldn't breathe. A pressure built up in her skull, sharp as a blade. Like the girl was trying to pry open Elaine's mind.

It felt like that *voice*, she realized, the one that had attacked after the first trial. Yet this was different, somehow. The prisoner's assault was archaic and crude where the rasp had been swift and methodical. A heartless butcher compared to a skilled surgeon.

Elaine fell to the floor. The noise was too much. It threatened to tear her apart from the inside out.

Then—

silence. Pure, blissful silence.

Elaine seized the reprieve and ran like her life depended on it, and she had the sneaking suspicion that it did. That if she had stayed there a moment longer, she would have broken.

And that, perhaps, someone had helped her escape.

CHAPTER 12

If the next trial asked her to describe her ceiling, Elaine would pass with flying colors. She had spent enough sleepless nights staring up at it to memorize every line, every groove, every shadow cast by the shifting moonlight. She didn't know which she doubted more: whether the next trial would actually ask for a description of her ceiling, or whether she would survive until then to find out.

After barely escaping the dungeon alive, Elaine had paced through the main drawing room. She had looked out the windows and waited for the others to return from the forest. When they finally emerged, the distance shrinking them to tiny ants in a green sea, she couldn't tear her eyes from Tether. He walked with Ava, their heads angled in lively conversation. He laughed at something she said. Elaine had never seen him laugh before; she had never seen him around anyone other than Jace.

They were probably talking about her. He was probably laughing at her. Fury burned a hole into the pit of her stomach, and she could still feel it now, red-hot and spiteful.

She tossed and turned in her bed. When she closed her eyes, she saw each of her nightmares clearly. That voice, whose ghost claws hadn't returned since last week. Finding herself buried under the dirt bed of the forest, unable to breathe, knowing that her family would die for her mistakes. And since venturing to the dungeon, she now had the shrieking prisoner to add to the list.

When she'd stumbled out of the hidden passage, hands clutching her scalp like her skull would shatter if she let go, a man she had never seen before was standing in the library. He gave her the slightest smile, the kind that said, *I know what you did, and I know what you found.* Only once she'd returned to her room did she put together that he must have been the same man who'd arrived in the car after the first trial.

She realized another thing, too. The strange tug that had led her to the dungeon, to the feral remnant of a girl—Elaine had felt it before. She recognized the rush of adrenaline and thrum in her veins like the glimmer of a memory. Then it dawned on her that she had felt that way around Lily. She'd almost thrown up when she made the connection.

That wasn't Lily down there. That couldn't have been Lily. Lily didn't look like that; Lily wouldn't act like that.

Elaine told herself this over and over and over like she was cooing a crying baby.

While she stayed awake that night waiting to be snatched from her bed and buried beneath evil trees, Elaine contemplated the many mysteries plaguing the castle. Who was that girl, where did the eliminated competitors go, who was that man from the car and what was he doing here, why did the ghost-woman behave so strangely, how did the trials seem to have technology more advanced than anything she had seen before...?

On and on she wondered, and on and on she came up blank for answers. Eventually, thinking about all the strangeness summoned a headache, and she quit trying to make sense of it.

The next day, the sun rose.

The sun rising might not have been a particularly significant event to most, but to Elaine it was nothing short of a miracle. A miracle that she could feel its warmth splay across her skin during training.

A miracle that she was not lying in a grave.

But her relief was short-lived. Her name hung trepidatiously at the bottom of the list, the very last rank—far from safe and close to being slashed in the next round of eliminations. If she failed the third trial—or did anything short of prodigious—not even fate could rescue her again.

"I can't believe he did that," Kate was saying at lunch. "Who breaks their arm just to get one person out? That's crazy."

It *was his shoulder*, Elaine almost corrected, *and he dislocated it*. But the words died on her tongue. She had no desire to recount her foolishness, and even less to marvel at Tether's brilliance.

"I think it was just a shoulder dislocation," Mason said. "I overheard him talking to Gino. Apparently he has this condition where he can't feel pain. Congenital analgesia, or something."

"Oh." Kate tore the last bit of meat from the bone. After she finished chewing, she said, "But still, it must have taken some effort to dislocate it in the first place. Why go through all the trouble just to get Elaine out?"

They both looked at her as if she had the answer. Elaine rolled her eyes and pushed her plate back. "I don't know."

The dining room bustled during lunchtime. Everyone spoke loudly, their voices bouncing off the wooden rafters and glass chandeliers. A far cry from the tired quiet of breakfast and somber silence of dinner.

"Does he hate you or something?" Kate tried again.

"I don't know. I'd never spoken to him before yesterday, so I don't see why he would."

"Who knows with him. The guy looks like he hates everyone. I wouldn't take it personally," Mason said in an attempt to be reassuring.

But to Elaine, it was personal. Tether had chosen her to punish for whatever twisted reason he'd conjured. Perhaps he *did* hate her. Or perhaps it had been nothing more than him noticing a weakness in her cringing at others' pain while watching the spars and seizing the opportunity to climb a rank.

It was personal to her, regardless of whether it had been personal to him. She was last. One wrong move and that cursed black slash would cross her name, too. One wrong move, and her family's only chance at survival would disappear like the eliminated competitors.

Alone in the bathroom that evening, Elaine made a promise to herself. She stared at her reflection in the mirror, at those sorrowful brown depths that she couldn't reconcile as her own eyes, and swore she would do whatever it took. The trials weren't fair; she needed to stop treating them like they were.

If she wanted to win, she had to play the game differently. She had to be as determined as Ava, as detached as Mason, as married to numbers as Gino, and as underhanded as Tether.

She had to lose herself to it.

CHAPTER 13

Elaine couldn't tear her eyes from the rankings. She couldn't *believe* the rankings, even a week later. Right there, with only three uncrossed names below it, was *Elaine Carter*. Her name—untouched by that cursed black line. Her gaze drifted downwards, to the ones who had not been so fortunate. The ones who had vanished that night.

She should have been among them. In her bones, she could feel fate toying with her. She had waited that night for somebody to drag her into the woods to the graveyard that no one had seen but everyone knew existed. That was where she was supposed to be. Yet, here she was. Alive.

Throughout the week after the second trial, Elaine had thrown herself at her classes. She woke up two hours before training—and many hours before the waning autumn sun would show its face—to pour over the stacks of books about chemistry and physics and battle tactics. In the evening, after most of the castle's lights had winked away, Elaine ran laps around the lawn until her breathing was ragged and her heart threatened to explode.

Her rank moved up—by three. A small victory, but an impressive one nonetheless. Ranks rarely shifted between trials. Besides, all it took was one person to fill her grave. Elaine flinched at the thought. How quickly had she accepted death?

Spars were her sole shortcoming. Since losing to Tether, Elaine had won three matches and lost seven. An embarrassing proportion made even more stark when she compared it to Mason's perfect record. After watching him win again, and not failing to note the distance in his gaze, an idea occurred to Elaine.

"Teach me how to fight," she said.

He almost smirked. "You want me to teach you to fight?" he repeated.

Elaine rolled her eyes. "You heard me."

The morning breeze twirled the loose strands of hair not looped into her braid. She shivered, hugging her jacket closer to her body.

"Meet me upstairs at the start of lunch," Mason said.

"Fifth floor?" She hated that godforsaken ballroom ever since that rasp had invaded her mind in it.

"Yeah. Where we had the first trial," he said. "It has enough space and you can watch yourself in the mirrors. Plus, no one will bother us up there."

She nodded. "See you then, sensei."

He chuckled as he receded down another hallway.

The ballroom door creaked when Elaine pushed it open as though annoyed at her for bothering it. She meant to leave it ajar for Mason, but the door swung shut on its own. The slam echoed off the decadent walls.

Elaine drifted into the heart of the ballroom. Silence sifted through the stale air. How long had passed without a dancer to bring life to the space? The ballroom seemed empty without bodies whose movements could match its beauty; it seemed lonely.

Without realizing it, Elaine began to sway on her feet. She lifted on her toes, raised her arms, and leaned back. Her body, each muscle that made her, remembered this dance the way her brain remembered the music. *Le Cygne*, The Dying Swan. Her arms, up and down: wings. She could practically hear the orchestra, growing sadder as the bird, the dancer, came to accept its death.

She froze when the door's hinges whined loudly, grateful for the warning. She willed her cheeks to stop burning at almost being caught.

"Hey," Mason said, stopping a few feet away. "I was thinking we should start with the basics today, and when you're ready we can practice sparring another time."

He dropped into a comfortable crouch and raised his arms protectively over his face. The way he did in the ring before every spar. For a split second, Elaine imagined herself as his opponent and flinched. If Mason noticed, he said nothing about it. "The key to these things is your stance. If you're balanced, it's a lot harder to get you on the ground." He gestured to his bent knees and leaned slightly forward. "Like this."

Elaine copied his positioning as best as she could, though it felt unnatural.

"You're too far forward," Mason said. "Lean back a little."

She listened, arching her back to the smallest degree. Her center strengthened and she readjusted her feet.

Mason nodded encouragingly. "Good. Now, a lot of times people remember good balance when they're on defense, but it's easy to forget when you attack."

He demonstrated an incorrect thrust. His feet shuffled awkwardly behind and he stumbled too far forward. "If you do that, your opponent can take advantage of you and use your momentum to throw you to the ground."

A trick she had used on others as often as it was used on her. "So how do you keep your balance, then?"

"Like this," he said, then launched himself at no one. He struck the air in a blow so fast Elaine barely saw it. "Focus on your core when you attack, not just your arms." He punched twice more for her to study, then stood back to watch her.

She attempted to mimic what he had done, but she was clumsy and uncoordinated where Mason had been swift and precise. She took a frustrated pause, ignored Mason's gaze, and tried again.

He stopped her. "You used to dance, didn't you?" He phrased it as a question, but he sounded certain in his assumption.

"How'd you know?"

"You move like a dancer," he said. "I used to have this friend who was trying to learn ballet. You have the same way of moving. She was actually dancing when she d—" Then he clamped his mouth shut.

They stared at each other awkwardly until he said, "Anyway, I think it might help to think of sparring as a dance. React to your opponent's moves the same way you would react to the beats of a song."

She practiced for the next half hour. Sometimes Mason would critique her, though more often he watched in silence, nodding when she executed the move correctly. By the end, a sheen of sweat covered her face and she had fought with the air more times than she could count.

"Tomorrow we'll work on spotting fake-outs," he said.

Every lunch Elaine climbed the endless steps to the fifth floor and practiced with Mason. He taught her basic footwork, spotting feigned attacks, and how to properly guard her face—hands up, elbows in, chin down. Then he showed her more complicated maneuvers: strikes and combinations, clinch work, and ground fighting. Once she mastered those, he instructed her on defending takedowns: sprawl by stepping one leg back and driving the hips forward to stuff the attempt, using underhooks to control the opponent's arms and disrupt their balance. He also demonstrated moves he didn't know the names of, which made Elaine wonder where he had learned them.

On the third day, they began sparring together. Elaine lost every match to him, as expected. She doubted she could ever beat Mason, even if she made it her life's mission. There was something too practiced about his movements, every parry and step too perfect. It unnerved her. No matter how clever she thought herself, she could never seem to take him off guard. It was as though he'd seen it all before.

By the third match, Elaine was wheezing. Mason dropped into a low stance, ready to start again.

She held up her hand. "I think I'm done for the day."

He straightened. "Alright."

Elaine lay on the ground and wound her fingers together over her stomach. The thousand crystals of the chandelier winked down at her, basking in the attention.

Mason sat next to her. "What do you think the next trial's going to be?"

"Who knows?" She certainly didn't. And if she did, she would never tell another soul, not even Mason.

Elaine considered her chances at passing the next day's eliminations. She had risen another rank yesterday, and now stood above Kate.

"Mason," she said, moving her head to look at him. Her cheek pressed into the cool wood. "You don't think I'm the reason Kate's so low, do you?"

He squinted at her as though she were speaking gibberish. "No, of course not. Why would you be?"

"When I got out, it was just Kate and Quinn left to defend the flag. I gave away the hiding spot." Elaine had thought about that moment too many times to count.

"It's not your fault," Mason said—insisted.

Elaine wanted to believe him. But it was her who'd fallen for Tether's trap. Her who'd allowed him to steal their flag.

"Elaine, it wasn't your fault, okay? Tether tricked you. You never meant to hurt anyone. And who even knows how they judge the trials? Kate's rank drop probably had nothing to do with you. And anyway, it's not like you came out unscathed. You're what, last? Second to last?"

She scoffed. "Thanks for the reminder."

"I'm serious. You should be more worried about yourself. Kate's fine. She's not your responsibility. We're all on our own here," he said, his tone abruptly cold. "If she can't handle it, that's her problem, not yours."

Elaine blinked at him. One moment, he would be laughing carelessly, smiling warmly. The next, he would be fighting mercilessly or telling her not to care about a friend dying. "If I got eliminated tomorrow, would you even care?" She couldn't help it. The words slipped through her lips without consent, biting, tinged with disgust.

Mason's face softened, realizing his mistake. "I didn't mean it like that. Of course I would."

"Sorry," Elaine said. "I know. You're right." She stood. "Thanks for helping me."

She won her match the next morning.

CHAPTER 14

As part of their study, Kron introduced another version of the Strategy Game. War with Allies, he called it. He assigned pairs—alliances and enemies. After each class, he would announce that day's players, and wait for them in this room after classes finished.

The day before the third trial, he called Elaine's name. "Gino and Kate are up against Elaine and Tether."

Tether stared at her from across the desks, and she could practically feel the disappointment rolling off of him. He thought she was weak. He thought that because he had fooled her once, she was stupid.

When she stepped into the darkened, empty classroom with the other three players, she promised herself she would not be weak or stupid. She would prove him wrong.

Kron had removed the desks, clearing the space for a massive war table plastered with a sprawling map on its face, the kind that would appear in movies where militants would shove their fingers onto the parchment and discuss battle plans over. She had no idea how he had managed to move all the desks out and lug in the massive piece of furniture in one afternoon, but supposed that with the help of a handful of servants it couldn't have been too arduous.

Her eyes flitted around the classroom. It looked different, and not just because the desks that had once cramped the space were gone. The curtains had been drawn shut, blocking any natural light, and the normally dead candles along the walls had been lit. The shifting darkness made the room larger and more grim.

Kron gestured for the two alliances to take up opposite sides of the table.

Elaine shifted as Tether stood still beside her. They looked over the terrain. Four markers of society: two kingdoms in the north and two kingdoms in the south. The continent took the shape of a pair of lungs turned sideways; a thin strip of land connected the two curving landmasses, the ocean carving a gap between them.

Elaine noted the various natural landmarks—mountains, rivers, lakes, deserts, wetlands, underground cave systems—as well as the fortresses and towns that dotted the map.

"Elaine, Tether," Kron said. "You are the Alliance of Yensal, composed of the Blue Republic and the Red Republic." He pointed to the two capitals on the northern landmass, one in the north and the other in the east. "You control this," he outlined the circular shape of the top landmass, "and these islands here." He pressed his thumb into a small spattering of land in the north of the *Green Sea*, as the map called it.

"Gino and Kate, you are the Alliance of Xor, composed of the Green Kingdom and Orange Kingdom." The Green Capital was in the northeast of the southern landmass, a coastal city bordering the sea of the kingdom's name, while the Orange capital lay to the west.

Elaine watched Kate study the layout of their battlegrounds. In order to win, Kate would have to lose. Which was unfortunate, as Kate was one of the few competitors she enjoyed speaking to, close enough to consider a friend. At least as close to a friend as one could get here.

Kate caught Elaine staring and bowed her head to such a small degree Elaine almost missed it. *No hard feelings*, the gesture said. No hard feelings, Elaine thought back. Win or lose.

But this was Strategy, and Elaine refused to lose.

Tether grabbed the wooden edge of the table and leaned on his arm. She stared at his hand for a moment before Kron's booming voice tore her attention away.

Kron continued, "You are at war with each other. The Xor Alliance drew first blood when trying to capture the Rig Islands of the Green Sea, claiming strategic trading ports along the southern coasts, though the Blue Republic still maintains control over much of the islands."

He brought out a tray containing red, blue, green, and orange figures that resembled toy soldiers and miniature flags of their colors to stick in the map and curved walls to serve as blockades, setting everything down on the table. He pinned four blue flags and thirteen red flags along the islands to mark the occupied ports.

"They start with more naval bases," Gino mumbled.

Kron heard him. "When have I ever taught you that war was fair?" Then he waved a hand over the map. "Xor has more soldiers anyway, so quit complaining."

Gino nodded. Nothing got under Kron's skin like whining.

Kron finished laying out all the soldiers across the map. "Begin."

At first, their moves consisted of defensive preparation. No one dared attack first while so exposed. Elaine set up medic camps along a few mountains where she predicted the major battles would occur based on the value of nearby fortresses. Tether had raised his eyebrows at that, but she quickly shut his protests down.

"It's not a waste of resources," she said. "We have fewer soldiers. Better to not have them all dying because *you* forgot to set up camps to heal them."

"Alright," he said, raising his hands in mock surrender. "What do you want, a pat on the back?"

"Just a competent partner," she muttered, but she could tell he heard. He peered at her in that same scrutinizing way he always did. And she stared right back, not bothering to temper the venomous hatred burning in her gaze.

He took in a sharp breath and turned away.

She had lied, in a sense; Tether was a competent partner. He had a good sense for where walls should go and where their armies would have the best chance of attacking from. But that did little to ease the sting of working with the person responsible for her fall in the ranks and her struggle to survive eliminations.

They put the final touches on their defense: a line of blockades to prevent a land campaign from the south and fortifying the more important ports on the mainland. If they lost those ports, they would lose their ships, too, and any chance at a naval offensive right along with them.

The map was quite the contraption, she found. When they decided where to place their armies, the surface would ripple, swallowing the toy soldiers and rendering them in the parchment itself. Elaine had leaped back in amazement the first time she witnessed it, though she hadn't bothered to ask Kron how it worked. Like the visions from the first trial and immobilizing shots from the second, this was simply another bizarre, unexplainable occurrence.

Each player had a small viewing station, a screen embedded into the wood at each corner that would zoom in on whatever portion of the map they selected. They could actually *see* the battles playing out, an option the solo Strategy Games had never offered. It would allow them to make more accurate decisions. It would also allow them to witness the bloodshed.

Elaine wondered what it would feel like to watch fake men chop each other to pieces because she ordered it.

Tether tapped his foot apprehensively. "We should attack them from the west," he whispered. "They haven't fortified it nearly well enough." The table was long enough that the opposing sides couldn't hear each other when they lowered their voices.

"I'll lend you two ships," she said.

"I need at least four."

Her republic had a stronger navy than his, though he had better numbers overall.

"Two," she insisted. "I'm using the rest to reclaim the islands."

He flexed his jaw. "If we don't succeed in the west, all we'll be doing is pointing out a weakness for them to fix."

"Fine, I'll give you three. But we need the islands to attack Green's capital. Our ships can't cross the whole way without stopping to refuel."

Despite Elaine's intent to attack first, Kate and Gino made the first move, Kate advancing her troops across the isthmus.

Elaine tried out the viewing porthole, selecting the area Kate's troops marched in. She saw lines and lines of bodies dressed in orange uniforms, weapons strapped to their backs. She saw the generals ordering their soldiers to chop the trees blocking their path, then saw men and women unsheathing axes and swinging.

She gawked at the verisimilitude of it. Everything looked so real, everyone so human. Each soldier had different features, a slightly different walk.

"Carter," Tether snapped, breaking her trance. "Focus."

Elaine glared at him, then made quick work of sending her ships off. She selected a coastal city to watch the gargantuan vessels disappear into the horizon.

As the war drew on, Elaine realized a funny thing about battles. They weren't isolated events as history books often tried to portray them. They were dominos, each cascading into the next toward an imminent end.

Their roles became clear with each battle that passed. Elaine fought on the southern landmass against Gino, who defended his capital. She pushed against his naval defenses with her superior fleet, finally blowing his last ship to bits and releasing her soldiers onto land to storm the city.

It took ten minutes to take the city, which felt like a lifetime of staring at swords clashing and cannons firing. Once each battle started, there wasn't much to do besides stand and watch. Elaine used the time to plan her next move, so that when Gino's troops finally attempted to retreat through a side entrance in the wall, she had archers stationed on her ship to kill them off.

Gino cursed under his breath. She could hardly hear him, but the sound pleased her. Gino was a boy of careful calculation. He thought in terms of numbers, strategized based on numbers, and acted on numbers. Emotion meant he had lost faith in the numbers.

For when Elaine had laid siege on his city, she had been outnumbered. And she had won.

Gino composed himself quickly. He called his troops to the north to form a barrier around Elaine. He knew the water around the gulf her ships were anchored in was too shallow to sail over. The rocks were steep enough to compromise the hulls. She wouldn't risk her ships by sailing around the coast, so she was stuck.

His troops marched forward, rows of soldiers and mobile cannons and archers farther back slowly choking Elaine's entry point until they fully surrounded the regions neighboring the city she held.

While Gino moved his soldiers, Elaine constructed canoes. Then she sent them off, vessels that could move, albeit slowly, through shallower water. Gino realized what she was doing and sent a squadron to stop the canoes from circling his flank from the coast.

At least, he thought he realized what she was doing.

In fact, the canoes rowing to the east wouldn't pose much of a threat to his army. They were empty, all connected by a sturdy rope and maneuvered by a single soldier—decoys. For each canoe that sailed around the coast, three more drifted in an underground cave system stretching from a coastal alcove all the way to the middle of the continent. Elaine placed five soldiers in each canoe navigating the cave system. They waited in a grotto until they all reached the end. By the time Gino saw her army gathering behind him, it was too late. Her soldiers slammed into his backlines, felling his archers while her cannons attacked him from the front.

He was forced to surrender in minutes.

Elaine turned her attention to the northern landmass. After Kate had overcome the blockade along the isthmus, a series of battles had led her and Tether to a stalemate in the valley between two mammoth mountains.

Elaine began mobilizing her troops to aid Tether's.

"Nice of you to finally join me," he said.

As Elaine's soldiers marched across the map, it became clear Kate didn't have much of a chance against the two of them. But then Kate did something peculiar. She retreated; not just away from the battle, but toward Elaine.

Elaine looked across the table at Kate, who offered a nod, and understood. Kate had accepted her fate, and if she was going to lose, she would rather lose to Elaine than lose to Tether.

She took little pleasure in conquering Kate's troops.

In the end, Elaine won. She had beaten Gino, beaten Kate, and, in a way, beaten Tether, too.

But she wasn't done.

Tether held out his hand for her to shake. "Nice work, partner," he said, expression not betraying anger at Kate's decision.

Elaine's smile was vicious. "Not so fast."

Without warning, boulders fell from the mountain her medic camp was stationed on, raining on Tether's troops. His viewing porthole was still trained on the scene. The boulders crumpled every last body until all that remained was rubble.

Gino and Kate watched on with wide eyes.

"What did you do?" Tether said, tone grim.

"I beat you," she answered sweetly.

"Can she do that?" Gino asked.

Kron studied the map.

"I still have some troops left at the camps," Tether said quickly. "I sent them there to heal."

Elaine tsked. "No, no. They're dead."

His hands balled into tight fists. "How."

"Poison." *Duh.* Why else would she have taken a detour in the rainforest?

"Whatever," Tether said. "You can't do that. We're in an alliance. The whole point of the game is that we fight together, not against each other. You broke the rules." He turned to Kron, who was still pondering his verdict.

"Didn't you do the reading?" Elaine asked Tether. His eyes narrowed, gaze growing deadly. "An alliance is only as great as fear of the enemy."

He understood then. She could tell by the way his nostrils flared.

"No enemy." She gestured to Kate and Gino's fallen armies. "No alliance." She smiled again for good measure, relishing in Tether's raging, shocked silence. *I win. You lose.*

"Brilliant," Kron said, dismissing them with a wave of his hand.

CHAPTER 15

A knock sounded at Elaine's door. She rubbed her eyes and tiredly slipped a sweater over her pajamas to answer it.

A servant stood outside her rooms, dressed in the usual plain gray garb, clutching a letter to his chest. "For Miss Elaine Carter," he said, holding the envelope out to her.

She thanked the servant as she plucked the envelope from his outstretched hands. The paper warmed her cold fingers. The servant nodded before hurrying down the hall.

She unfolded the letter. It contained instructions for the coming trial. She frowned at the servant's receding figure. Whoever governed the competition had a flair for dramatics: letters delivered in the darkness before dawn, the vanishing act of an elimination, even hosting the trials in an ancient castle. Everything pointed to a person fond of spectacle, a person the ghost-woman was not.

Elaine shut the door to change into more suitable clothes to head downstairs in. She glanced once more at the parchment before leaving. It had a yellow tint to it, like papyrus. She noted the strange heat pulsing through it as if it were alive.

Life is precious, she thought for no reason at all, two ideas suddenly crashing together. *Paper is precious.*

Elaine stuffed the paper in her pocket instead of tossing it aside.

The letter said that the third trial would begin in the dining room. By the time Elaine arrived, ten others had taken their seats. The rest of the competition trickled in soon after.

Elaine was well aware that this trial could be her last. Her rank held little promise of escaping elimination. But if she was doomed, she would at least go out with a fight.

The ghost-woman slid into the room through the servants' entrance when the clock struck six. Her tone, as always, communicated an inexhaustible boredom that grated against Elaine's ears.

"Among other virtues, this trial will test your ability to survive with limited resources. You will not have a flare. You will not be able to call for help. You will not be allowed back into the castle without a key. The trial will last until Sunday night." As she spoke, three servants fanned out to distribute brown rucksacks.

"Your bag contains a compass, a bottle, and a box of matches. Your compass will not work around others. If you get thirsty, unstop the bottle. It will pull the moisture out of the air. Its contents will be safe to drink. You are on your own to secure food and shelter."

One of the servants dropped a bag into Elaine's arms and flitted away. The ghost-woman waited until the servants left to say gravely, "You may not under any circumstance harm another competitor." For if they were left together in the wilderness without supervision, murder wouldn't be so far a stretch. Unless, of course, it broke the rules.

"Return with your key, or don't return at all."

Find your key, or die.

CHAPTER 16

Death had never been an option in the previous trials. Nor had starvation, or finding yourself hopelessly lost in the woods, or being eaten alive by wild predators.

Now they were.

Elaine shoved away her morbid thoughts and rummaged through her bag. Bottle—check. Matches—check. Compass... She pulled out a rock instead. No, not a rock, she realized when she held it up to the growing morning light. A crystal. A clear crystal the size of a baby's fist, with blood-red veins snaking inside. Either her bag was faulty or this rock was the compass and would somehow lead her to a key.

She scanned the treeline. A few lingered by the castle, hesitation wrought in their pause, but the majority of competitors had already left. Instead of following, Elaine darted into the gardens. Night had shrouded her vision the last time she had visited the gardens returning from the woods with Mason, but Elaine had noticed brambles brimming with berries. Weeks had passed since then. She hoped there might still be some fruit left.

Scrawny vines clung to the garden walls, adorning the arched entrance like a suffocating necklace. Birds chirped from the high canopy of leaves that shaded the stone pathway. She passed the gushing fountain at the center of the garden. A grin pulled at the corners of her lips when she beheld the spattering of red on the far side of the garden. Elaine made quick work of collecting the raspberries. Once she had cleared the brambles of their fruit, she sprinted into the forest, anxiety pounding in her skull.

She hated the woods. She hated it, hated it, hated it beneath the spindly trees that blocked the sun from reaching the ground and echoed the eerie cacophony of hidden creatures.

The crystal weighed heavy in her hand. As she passed a fallen branch, it began to throb. It was a subtle thing, a faint rhythmic fluttering that vibrated against her palm. She held the crystal up. A faint glow pulsed in sync with the steady rise and fall of the murmuring. As she neared the branch, it grew brighter and louder, though still unassuming if one wasn't paying close attention.

It beat urgently when she neared the end of the branch. She crouched to peer into the hollow body of wood. Brown leaves lined the floor, rustling as Elaine reached a hand inside. Leaf, dirt, more leaf, pebble, something slimy—she blanched—twig, hard object.

She pulled out a shiny gold square with the thickness of a puzzle piece. An orange border on the top and right sides made Elaine think this was the corner of a larger square.

The phrase, *Ponder your g—*, was cut off.

She squinted at the words before stowing the piece in her bag and moving further into the forest. A long while passed before the crystal lit up again. This second time was different, more explosive. The crystal glowed brightly, rays of white light spilling between her fingers. Its trill was louder, too, filling Elaine's ears and blocking the sounds of the forest. It led her to where scraggly roots bunched up at the base of a large tree.

Elaine dropped to her knees and held the crystal in front of her. It flashed as it got closer to the ground. Her eyebrows drew together until she noticed a gap between the roots that burrowed into the forest floor.

The crystal illuminated the hole, and she could make out—

A *hiss* was her only warning for what happened next. A striped snake lunged at her from the darkness. Elaine cried out and fell on her elbows. The crystal rolled from her grasp. Sharp teeth pierced the skin of her calf. She gasped as the snake's fangs sunk into her flesh.

Then it was gone, slithering away. Breathing heavily, Elaine sat up and inspected the wound. Two wells of red began to drip down her leg. She cursed and tried to remember the children's rhyme about venomous snakes. What was it again? *Red touches yellow, kills a fellow,* or something like that. Elaine hadn't seen yellow stripes, but in her distress she could have missed such a detail. *Don't panic,* she told herself. If the snake had been poisonous, there was nothing she could do about it now.

She reached the crystal into the pit and used its light to see, certain a piece was down there. Sure enough, gold shined at her from under a pile of leaves. This time, no snake attacked when Elane stuck her arm down.

This square's border was a different color than the last one: red, not orange. The same red as the seams in her crystal. When she sat the two pieces next to each other on the ground, they melded together. Elaine gasped. It was like watching a gash stitch together at an unnaturally fast rate, except instead of skin it was metal.

The entire border became red, color leaching from the new piece into the first. Red was her color, apparently. Which meant that the first piece she'd found belonged to someone else.

Ponder your greatest was centered—

Branches snapped behind her and Elaine shoved the gold slab into her bag. The rule prohibited harming one another, not stealing.

"Elaine?"

She let out a sigh of relief at Kate's voice. "Over here," she called out.

Kate regarded her resting on the floor with confusion. "Are you alright? I heard shouting."

"I'm fine," Elaine replied, though the skin around the bite felt tender. "A snake bit me."

"A snake?"

Elaine twisted her leg so that Kate could see the injury. "Yeah. But I don't think it was venomous," she added upon noticing the expression of appall on her friend's face.

"O—Okay. If you say so," Kate said, moving to help Elaine stand.

"Have you found any pieces yet?" Elaine asked to fill the silence. And to gauge if she was behind or not.

Kate nodded. "One."

"Can I see your crystal?"

Kate pulled the odd compass out of her bag. "Sure."

Their crystals were identical, except for their streaks of color. Kate's had the delicate pink hue of budding flowers at springtime.

Kate noticed the parchment sticking out of Elaine's pocket. "What's that?"

Elaine's gaze flicked from the jewel to the finger pointing at her hip. "Oh," she said, unfolding the paper. "It's the letter from earlier..." Her voice drifted upon noticing the crooked streaks of ink.

"That's not the letter," Kate said unnecessarily.

To Elaine's bewilderment, she held a map instead of the letter she had packed. Gone was the cursive scrawl dictating the trial's schedule. In its place, black ink carved out a map of the forest. Exaggerated curves indicated the ocean.

"We came from here, right?" Elaine prompted, indicating to the right corner of the blank rectangle she assumed was the lawn.

"I think so."

"And we went this direction..." She dragged her finger up along the map. "I think...I think we're somewhere around here." She paused to look at Kate. "What do you say we meet up at the coast? It looks like there's a lighthouse there. That way we have somewhere to sleep and we can help each other make dinner."

"Sure," Kate agreed, but not before asking. "How'd you know to bring the letter?"

"I don't know. I just thought it seemed weird," Elaine said with a shrug, pocketing the parchment.

They agreed which paths they would take to the coast before splitting up.

By nightfall, Elaine had found three of the four pieces. She contemplated forgoing the plan of staying overnight at the lighthouse to continue searching, but her stomach wrenched in pain. She checked her pack—the berries were nothing more than red smears across fabric.

Besides, she could already see the lighthouse.

The lighthouse sat idly on a cliff, the dark ocean crashing against rocks below. Despite its function, the tall white spire didn't release a lick of light. It was hardly visible except for the copper tip that captured the faint glow of the moon.

Elaine shivered violently. Fire, she thought. They needed to start a fire before hypothermia set in.

"There you are!" Kate exclaimed, coming out from a door that was falling off its hinges.

"Can you gather wood?" Elaine asked. "I'm going to try to find food, and when I get back I'll help you start a fire. Make sure the pieces you choose are dry."

Kate nodded and set off into the woods.

Elaine found a wild apple tree and plucked some of the low-hanging fruit, keeping her eyes peeled for any animals she could snare. She waited patiently by a stream, clutching a rock tightly.

The forest teemed with life, hosting more animals than Elaine could count. It was only a matter of time before a large quail waddled to her, unaware of the hunter lying in wait.

She made sure to give the bird as painless a death as she could.

When she returned, Kate had already started a fire. Smoke drifted skywards. The flames licked at the blackening wood, embers flying in the darkness. Elaine sat on the grass next to Kate and lifted her hands over the fire.

Elaine glanced at Kate, who stared at the quail lying at the ground with disgust. "How many pieces do you have?" Elaine asked.

Kate looked up from the quail. "Two. You?"

"Three."

As Kate drifted to sleep, Elaine whispered, "You know, you remind me of someone." She said it so quietly she wasn't sure Kate heard.

But Kate smiled drowsily. "That's nice."

Elaine tilted her head up at the sky. The stars gazed back at her, a thousand glimpses into the past, a thousand relics of other worlds. And somewhere among them, the Fall headed towards Earth.

Elaine used to look at the night sky and see beauty and possibility, feel hope in her chest like a warm, glowing flower unfurling its petals. Now, she saw only death and felt a thick dread coating her insides like poison.

CHAPTER 17

When Elaine awoke, bruised light hid the stars. The fire was nothing but blackened twigs.

She nudged Kate's shoulder before leaving. Kate mumbled something in her sleep, curling into a ball. "Wake up, Li—" She caught herself before uttering her sister's name, but she couldn't stop herself from seeing Lily in Kate. Asleep, Kate looked like Lily had dead. Peaceful. Innocent. Undeserving of her fate.

"Wake up," she said, louder this time.

Kate's eyes finally opened, and she sat up. "Morning," she murmured.

"We should get going," Elaine said. "It'll be easier to find our pieces if it's dark."

They parted ways again so that their compasses would work. Elaine found her last piece before the sun rose, tucked high in the branches of a shedding maple tree. She almost fell onto her head trying to reach it.

She climbed down, set the gold L-shaped piece onto the ground and watched as the square completed itself. Thin metal tendrils slithered from the edges, intertwining with the new piece.

Once the square was complete, the phrase read: *Ponder your greatest hope.*

Then Elaine felt the gold tug her. It physically pulled her arms forward. She stumbled, catching herself.

"Elaine?"

She spun around. Mason nodded to her map. "You're finished?"

She considered him. "You can come with me if you want, as long as I get to go first," Elaine suggested. She trusted him. "I owe you for the sparring lesson anyway."

"Fair enough."

Elaine held onto the golden square as it dragged her towards some known end. Mason trailed behind.

Ponder your greatest hope. Elaine turned the words over in her mind. Her greatest hope? The Fall never existing at all. Henry safe. Holding Lily in her arms again. Her throat clenched. Impossible. Lily was gone and buried, dead, and yet—Elaine could feel her now closer than ever, her ghost. She felt Lily in these woods, in that castle.

"We're getting close," Mason said, more to himself than to her.

A distant chuckle had them spinning around. "I don't think that's going to work, Carter."

"What do you mean?" Mason called out.

"I'm under the impression we have to trade in our gold for the key." Tether's blue eyes twinkled as he added, "I don't think there's a boyfriend-girlfriend special."

Elaine couldn't help but roll her eyes. "How do you know?"

Tether raised his eyebrows. "About the bo—"

She interrupted him through gritted teeth. "You know what I mean. About how we trade our gold for our key."

"You see that lake over there?" he asked, gesturing to a pool of water past a line of trees. "There's a box at the bottom. The water's so clear you can see all the way down. The box has a slot. I think it's for the square we put together."

"How come you haven't got your key already?" Mason asked from beside her.

Tether smirked. "Who says I haven't?"

Annoyance etched lines between Elaine's brows. "Because you're still standing here like an idiot," she interjected, then faced Mason. "Let's see for ourselves. Maybe he's wrong."

She heard a faint tsk.

Sure enough, a wooden box sat some five hundred feet below the surface of the water, idly waiting to be fed gold. "I guess I better go," Mason said, shoulders slumped. He shrugged it off after a moment. "See you later."

Elaine gave him a sad smile as if to say, *Sorry* and *Good luck.*

Then he ran off with a quickness Elaine envied.

"Are you going to try to swim now?" Tether asked.

Elaine slowly turned around, pointing out the obvious. "I can't hold my breath five hundred feet down and five hundred feet up."

"I used to dive competitively, when I was younger," Tether started, and the image of a little him atop a diving board almost made her laugh. "And even I don't think I could make it all the way down."

She let out a frustrated sigh. What was the point, traveling through an animal-infested forest, getting bitten by a snake, surviving freezing temperatures, eating half-raw quail meat, finding all the pieces, only to be stopped by the shortcoming of human lungs?

The lake magnified the silence with its stillness. "Wait a second," Elaine thought aloud. "You hear that?"

"Hear what?"

"Exactly. It's quiet here—too quiet. Haven't you noticed how many animals there are around here?" she went on. Tether nodded, beginning to understand her logic. "Shouldn't they be at this lake, drinking at the only source of freshwater for miles?"

"You think this isn't actually water," Tether finished for her.

Elaine's answer was to retrieve the bottle from her pack and kneel at the edge of the lake. She dumped out the liquid from earlier and quickly covered the opening so that it wouldn't refill itself. Then she lowered the vial face down, only slipping her hand away once the glass rim kissed the surface of the lake.

She held her breath. So did Tether, who had come to stand next to her. To their collective astonishment, the bottle's magic didn't pull any of the water up. Which meant that, somehow, this lake wasn't actually composed of water.

"Brilliant," Tether whispered, a noise Elaine wished didn't warm her the way it did.

She stood, suddenly realizing how close they were when his breath fanned over her forehead. She took a step back.

"You go first," he said.

"Because you're being nice or because you want to see if I choke on the stuff before you get in?"

"Can't it be a little bit of both?" he said, flashing a charming smile.

"Whatever," she mumbled.

"I'll save you if you start to choke," he promised.

Elaine glanced at him as she pulled out the golden slate and dropped her pack to the ground. "Sure you will," she replied sarcastically.

Before Tether could spew out any other nonsense, she dove into the water.

A splash, and then—cold. Freezing cold all around her. The kind of cold that stung one's skin like an army of angry bees. The deeper she swam, the colder it got. And when she tried to breathe, she couldn't. The liquid caught in her throat, blocking her airway. She gasped and began to cough, but that only allowed more of the liquid into her mouth.

Desperation had made her stupid. She should have tested her theory closer to the surface. Here, even as panic drove her to swim up, she would drown before she reached air.

She thought she heard a splash. She might have seen arms reaching for her from above. But then the most peculiar thing happened: she took a breath. She breathed, hesitantly at first, then greedily. She gulped down the oxygen until her lungs forgave her, until she was strong enough to continue swimming.

It was something out of a dream, to feel water rushing around one's body but to see clearly and breathe deeply. Elaine smiled against the cold, which at once felt comforting.

The dirt flew around her as she landed beside the chest. It looked like it belonged to another time, where a band of pirates would embark on a quest to find it.

A slit waited patiently for her to feed it the gold slate. Elaine obliged, gently fitting the square into the gap. For a moment, the chest was still. A swell of current tussled with her hair, brown strands rising like flames above her head. Then the chest rumbled, enveloping the map. Elaine could hear nothing but the depth.

Ponder your greatest hope, Elaine, a deep voice echoed in her skull, as though the chest was speaking to her. She paused, lost in thought. *Lily.* Seeing her sister's rosy cheeks again, chubby and smiling. Her hazel eyes crinkled in happiness. Her arms around Elaine's middle like they were on the rare days they weren't fighting.

But the chest rejected that. Lily wasn't her greatest hope—Lily was dead. So Elaine thought of Henry, of holding him in her arms that day in the hospital, wishing he hadn't been born to a doomed world.

The chest spoke again. *That is not your greatest hope. Why are you here, Elaine?*

Here, at the bottom of a lake not full of water, but something else. Here, at the top of a mountain perpetually shrouded in fog. Here, competing to protect her family.

Here, fighting to atone for being the reason her sister died.

There it was, her greatest hope: being the reason Henry was safe. Finally becoming someone worthy of love, deserving of life. Someone she had not been for far too long.

Redemption.

The chest let out something of a satisfied sigh. The rusted silver clasp twisted, and the chest opened its mouth wide, revealing a blood-red key. The metal glinted in the light that filtered through the surface of the lake, winking at her. *You found me*, it seemed to say.

I found me, too, she thought, before grabbing the key and launching to the surface.

CHAPTER 18

For the first time in a long time, Elaine was happy. Blissfully happy. So happy, that upon breaking the surface of the lake, she hardly registered that she was choking. She was smiling as her throat constricted and as arms wrapped around her waist and hauled her to shore.

"Elaine!" someone said.

She blinked away the haze and found herself staring into bright, worried eyes. Assuming the worst of her silence, Tether pressed his palms into her sternum and began to apply pressure.

"Ow," Elaine exclaimed, shoving his hands away. "I'm fine, I'm fine! I don't need CPR."

Tether leaned back on his heels. "You were choking," he said dumbly.

"I was just getting used to breathing normal air again, I think," she tried to explain, though she didn't quite understand it herself.

They sat in silence while her breathing slowed to a regular rhythm.

"What's that?" he asked suddenly, gesturing to her leg. Elaine glanced at the makeshift bandage wrapped around her calf, now soaked through. A pinprick of red had bled through the fabric.

"A snake bit me."

"Oh." He paused, then said with a note of concern that made Elaine wonder if the liquid in the lake had messed with her brain, "Are you okay? Was it venomous?"

She shook her head. "I doubt it. I'm still here, aren't I?"

Tether stared at the bandage for another beat of silence, then shifted his gaze to the treasure chest below crystal waters. "When you went down there, what did you think about?" *What is your greatest hope?*

Elaine shrugged, as though the question meant nothing. As though she hadn't bared her soul, raw and bleeding, to get that key. "Same thing as everyone else. Making it past eliminations, keeping my family safe." A half-truth, at least.

Tether nodded, though by the flick in his jaw Elaine could tell something bothered him.

"See you back at the castle?" he asked when she stood, tone almost hesitant.

She smiled sweetly. "Only if my luck runs out."

His laugh followed her as she ran to the castle, key clenched in a tight fist.

Unlike Elaine's return from the last trial, when her ears burned with shame, the castle's quiet didn't taunt her this time. It congratulated her. It spoke of victory.

She had been the first to give the ghost-woman her key. She had won.

Elaine waltzed through the perfectly empty halls. She lingered in the main drawing room, peering at the ghost-woman on the lawn below, who stood eerily still as she waited for the competitors to turn in their keys.

Elaine eyed the forest. The ones who failed to retrieve their keys, would the ghost-woman lock them out? Let them starve in the wilderness? Or would they instead be cut down once time ran out? There wasn't much of a difference either way, she supposed.

Tether crossed the lawn and dropped his key in the vase by the ghost-woman's feet. As if sensing her stare, he glanced up. An excited hum filled her ears when their gazes met.

He appeared behind her moments later, hair still damp from the lake, and fell onto the couch closest to the window. "Tell me something, Carter."

She turned to him. "What?"

He watched her closely as he asked, "What do you make of all this?"

"All what?" she said.

"This." He waved a hand through the air, at the ghost-woman below, at the forest beyond the glass. "The castle, the trials, everything. Don't you think it's weird?"

"Of course I do," she bit out, slightly annoyed at entertaining this conversation. Slightly annoyed that she enjoyed his company. "Everyone thinks it's weird." And they hadn't even found the screaming girl encaged beneath their feet or heard voices in their heads.

Tether leaned his elbows onto his legs and sat forward. "I think something else is going on. Something bigger than us. Bigger than the Fall, even."

"Nothing's bigger than the Fall," she retorted.

He shrugged absentmindedly as if it made no difference to him either way. "If you say so."

Standing near him made her head spin. After a simmering silence entrenched itself between them, Elaine mumbled, "I'm going to go lay down," and left the room. She felt hot and itchy all over. That may have been why, instead of turning left into the staircase that went to the third floor, she walked straight for several paces until the hallway abruptly ended.

She blinked dizzily at the wall. *That's weird*, she thought. She could've sworn the castle was wider than this.

The wood grain of the wall swirled. She tried to shake it away, but her vision continued to waver. The burning faded along with her lightheadedness. Suddenly, she understood what she was looking at.

A stereogram. Her favorite puzzle. She stepped back and stared at the wood until the image revealed itself. The wooden grain shifted into an arrow that pointed toward a singular point at the bottom of the wall. Elaine made a mental mark of the location before moving to crouch beside the wall, running her fingers over the area. Smooth wood, and then—*click*.

A camouflaged button sunk into the wood.

The wall rumbled and slid away to reveal a dark room. Elaine forgot to hesitate before walking in. The door closed behind her, too fast to escape without the threat of being crushed, and thrust her vision into black.

She almost screamed for help.

But then the room flickered to life.

CHAPTER 19

Every surface was a screen—the walls, the ceiling, and even the floor. For a moment, the room was suspended in a low strum, still but not quite peaceful, like the calm before a storm.

Then the screens flashed a blinding light and Elaine was transported to another world. Or rather, many worlds. Each screen showed the scene of a place that was distinctly not Earth. On the wall in front of her, a red desert was littered with bodies. Gray-scaled creatures lay in piles, teal blood spilling across the sand. Elaine shrunk back, but she couldn't escape the destruction.

To her right, an explosion tore through a tall dam. Water erupted from its cage. Elaine thought it would crush her. The camera zoomed out, focusing on a nearby city. The water ran through a valley, consuming whatever farmland or house stood in its way. Then it was upon the city. She held her breath; she swore she could hear faint screaming above the electric whir. Waves crashed upon the buildings, tearing them down.

She averted her gaze but was met with an even more gruesome scene on the ceiling. Explosions and fire reigned over the towns in the background. The camera was focused on a singular carriage. A woman smeared in blood rode the horse pulling it, desperation written in the whites of her knuckles as she held the reins tightly and in the way her eyes couldn't stay still.

Elaine stumbled back as an arrow knocked the woman off her saddle. A man jumped out of the moving carriage, landing in a puddle of muck. He crawled to the woman, and the camera followed. It zoomed in on his face; he seemed to be wailing.

A cloaked figure entered the frame. Elaine saw it before the man did. Too focused on his dead companion, the man only noticed the newcomer when the hood blocked the moonlight. Even then, he didn't seem startled, or even afraid—his eyes were hollow with loss.

The two stared at each other in what seemed like conversation, except their mouths didn't move. Then, without warning, the cloaked figure chopped off the man's head with a blade concealed in the folds of its robe.

Elaine swore she heard a rasp tickling her ear. She gasped and finally looked away, but the images surrounded her. Death and destruction covered every surface. Blood. Fire. Floods. Swords. Bombs.

She shut her eyes and banged on the wall she had entered through. Her head swam.

Thankfully, as though hearing her internal screams, the door slid open to release her.

———

Competitors returned from the forest in waves. The solitary ones were lucky. As the hours ticked toward sundown on the last day, it became more common to see groups. Two, three, or four coming out of the trees at the same time, realizing they were not alone, and sprinting across the lawn to reach the ghost-woman first despite their hunger and exhaustion. Some fainted, dropping like flies on the grass, before they could finish the trial.

Six never emerged from the woods at all.

Elaine's heart dropped as the sun slumped lower and lower, and Kate had still not returned. She imagined Kate stumbling through darkness, clothes snagged by skeletal branches, a girl barely out of childhood…

But before the last rays were swallowed by the trees on the horizon, Kate's figure appeared on the lawn. Elaine sighed with relief.

Kate was shaking when Elaine found her in the gardens. "I'm out," she said, expression frozen in a sort of horrified shock. "I'm really done for."

There was nothing Elaine could say to refute that, because Kate had finished the trial last—and barely at that. Partly because Kate was so terrified, and partly because of her own curiosity, Elaine agreed to stay in Kate's room that night.

Kate rested her head on a pillow beside Elaine's lap. "I'm not going to die, am I?" she whispered. Even having taken on the role as her family's protector, Kate still sounded like a child. A scared child with questions about the future that no one had answers to.

"No," Elaine assured her, despite not knowing. "You're not going to die."

"You'll stay here all night?" Kate looked up, wide eyes glazed over with tears.

"I'll stay here all night," Elaine promised. Perhaps it was unnecessary—perhaps Kate would pass eliminations by a hair's breadth and everything would be all right. Unlikely, but possible. Elaine had passed the last elimination when the odds were against her. Yet somehow she felt that it would be different for Kate.

"Every now and then my compass would light up," Kate said. "It was so random. It made it hard to find other people's pieces, too." She laughed, a fluttery, depressed noise that caused a lump in Elaine's throat. "You know why? Someone had tied my piece to a bird. It kept flying over my head. I barely caught it. Isn't that so stupid? I'm going to die because of a bird."

It was ingenious. Selfish, cruel—and terribly clever. The pieces were indestructible: fires couldn't burn them, force couldn't tear them, water couldn't soil them. If you tried to hold onto an extra piece, it would dematerialize and reappear somewhere else. But the gold slates were light. Tying them to a creature was the only way to make them harder to find.

Kate seemed to hate the silence. It probably carried the muted warning of death. She filled it with her hushed voice. "You said I reminded you of someone. Tell me about them. Please," she added when Elaine hesitated.

"My sister. You talk like her, a little, and you have the same hair." A pause. "You're around her age, actually." If Lily had lived this long, that was.

"You seem like you'd make a good sister," Kate said absentmindedly.

Irony was a knife twisting in Elaine's chest.

Elaine awoke with a start. Kate's room—she was in Kate's room, not her own. Yet the bed was empty. She was alone.

Kate was gone.

Elaine flew out of the armchair. "Kate?" she called, frantic. "Kate, are you there?"

No one answered. Denial rooted her feet to the carpet. Resentment paralyzed her. How could she fall asleep? How could she let Kate be taken? The logical part of Elaine's brain recognized that someone else was to blame. Stranger things than artificially-induced sleep had happened in this castle. But the other part of Elaine, the part marred in scars from Lily's death, the part that would never forgive herself for failing to save her sister—that part was louder.

You can't protect anyone. She couldn't halt her spiraling thoughts. Lily, Kate. Who was next? Henry? How was she supposed to fight the Fall, defend humanity, when all she did was fail to save the people closest to her?

She glanced at Kate's clock. Ten minutes until she had to be down on the lawn, running and jumping and sparring and pretending nothing had happened, acting like her friend hadn't just died.

She hoped she wouldn't cross paths with the ghost-woman on her way to her room to get changed. She hoped she wouldn't look too hard at Tom or the servants and wonder what role they played in the disappearances. If she did any of those things, she might lose her temper. She might scream—about the blood on their hands, about how unfair it was to torture children with unspoken threats of secret graves lying in wait.

Screaming would be a terrible idea. Elaine kept her head down during the laps, focused on the soreness of her muscles, and pushed aside any thoughts of Kate.

Tom introduced a new unit to training that day: target practice. Guns lay on the grass in a long row. And not the ones they used during capture the flag. Real guns. With real bullets. One for each competitor. Elaine swallowed tightly. She picked one up, weighed it in her hands. Hated the ease with which she held it. A weapon of destruction, fitting so perfectly in the curve of her palm. She wondered if this was how the war would go, too. If she would be scared of the carnage, at first, then accept it. Then become numb to it.

Then enjoy it. Or the Fall might kill her before she reached that point.

Such jolly thoughts, she deadpanned internally.

It was far too cold to be outside, especially since the sun hadn't yet thawed the autumn night's chill. Elaine lamented leaving her heavier jacket behind with a shiver.

"Take a target!" Tom ordered.

The targets—dummies painted to highlight weak points—stared at them lifelessly from across the lawn. They didn't flinch when the bullets pierced fabric, but Elaine did. Even though hers went careening into some ill-fated tree, not the intended marks.

She glanced to the target to the right of hers. A perfect hole, straight through the head's bullseye. Mason didn't seem surprised by his accuracy. Rather, Elaine noticed after the next few shots, he seemed to expect it. Ava was the only one who came close to his proficiency, nine of her shots hitting bullseyes.

"Where did you learn to use that so well?" Elaine asked as they walked back inside, gesturing to where his gun lay on the ground. Her dummy had gotten lucky—she landed a single shot on the edge of its shoulder. Mason's, on the other hand, had died ten times over.

"This whole thing's so stupid," he said, as though he hadn't heard her speak. But Elaine had seen his eyes shift at her question. He'd heard her. "The Fall won't even look human. They'll have different weak spots. What's the point of practicing on a human form?"

"How do you know? What if they do look human?" Elaine hadn't meant to sound aggressive, but Mason dodging her previous question had set her on edge.

Mason lifted his eyebrows. "Come on, Elaine. What are the chances, that out of an infinite number of possibilities of how they could look, the Fall would look like us?"

"Whatever," Elaine mumbled. "Training's probably just trying to desensitize us to violence. That's why we're using guns." *Though it seems some of us are already desensitized.* Elaine remembered how unaffected Mason looked while pummeling his opponents in the ring.

He shook his head, light hair swaying. "I just don't see the point. We don't know anything about them. We barely have the technology to meet them in battle—and they've managed to figure out long distance space travel." Bitterness laced his tone. "What's even the point in trying? They're just going to kill us all, and we won't stand a chance."

"We have to try," Elaine said, though her words rang hollow.

She had to believe they stood a chance. She had to hope. She couldn't face the truth. That humanity, no matter how tall they stood, no matter that they had conquered an entire planet, could fall.

Yet fall they would.

"That was you? I heard about that..." Elaine heard Jace saying.

When Tether responded, her blood ran cold. "Yeah, I tied like six pieces to the finches. Can you imagine the look on their faces? I wished I could've seen whoever ended up chasing a bird around the forest. They must've looked so moronic." He laughed smugly before he noticed Elaine watching.

Then he went quiet.

"Elaine." Mason tried to hold her back, but she tore her arm from his grasp.

She marched over to Tether, face burning in anger, hands balled in fists at her sides. She tilted her head up to stare at him straight in the eyes. His friends stopped talking.

"Shut up," she said.

He leaned in closer, as though to taunt her. "Why?" A whisper for her ears only.

"*Why*? Do you not care that those kids are probably dead?" Her voice rose as it broke. "I get why you *did* it. You want to win. That's fine. What I don't get is how you think it's *funny* that you sent a bunch of kids to their graves. Are you a *psychopath*? Are you brain damaged?"

She might as well have hit him. He reared back, a stricken expression contorting his face.

But he recovered quickly. "Get over yourself, Carter."

CHAPTER 20

The fourth trial took place in the chemistry lab.

All thirty-five remaining competitors filed into the space and claimed a station. Elaine wound up at the front, close enough to the ghost-woman to make out her slight frown.

The ghost-woman addressed them, her voice carrying its usual notes of boredom and indifference. "Each lab station has a book describing the experiment. You may only use the equipment at your station. There should be no problem with this. You will find you have everything you need. You may not tamper with another person's experiment. You have six hours to complete the assignment."

Good luck, Elaine added for the ghost-woman, who promptly departed.

Elaine opened the book and began to read. "Poison," she whispered to herself. The instructions were roundabout and succinctly vague, but the task was clear.

For the fourth trial, they would develop poison. The poison, if alchemized correctly, should be fatal even in the smallest doses to a fictionalized species and harmless to humans. The lab book briefly described the fictionalized species as similar to humans, essentially genetic cousins of Homo sapiens, though there were a few marked differences that the chemistry would exploit.

She started to organize the reactants and materials on her desk. Based on her skimming of the experiment, the actual reactions would take four hours. She tried to read more carefully, searching for steps that could be shortened, but found that she knew too little to properly work around the instructions. If only their chemistry class hadn't wasted a month on agricultural chemistry.

Elaine weighed her two options: start now, or plan the steps first. She chose the latter without much hesitation. Forethought tended to pay its dividends. She eyed the stack of books with additional information about the experiment, sighed, and brought them to the desk behind her bench. She began cross-referencing the more complicated steps outlined in the instructions with the extra texts.

It took an entire half hour to figure out a shortcut she could make, and another ten minutes for the next. But, not only did the shortcuts save time overall, they would yield a purer product. She left the references face-up and finished writing the reactions out. She glanced up at the clock. Four hours and forty-nine minutes left. She looked around; most of the others were either well into their work or already getting started.

Miranda, who had started mixing and boiling chemicals the moment the timer started, was many steps ahead. Elaine didn't let herself panic. She started measuring the amount of calcium she would need, placing the fine powder on the scale, adding and removing depending on the number displayed.

To her right, Tether stood motionless at his desk, still reading the different texts.

Elaine carefully mixed two reactants in a boiling flask with a magnetic stirrer. While that solution combined, she started on the other two processes that could be done simultaneously. Together, they would create a reagent for a future step of the primary reactions.

Her legs grew tired. After two hours, with the last hour spent shifting from one foot to another, standing at her bench became unbearable. Her head swirled from focusing on the different burbling liquids—and possibly also from inhaling the many chemicals wafting through the air.

Just as Elaine was about to leave the room to sit down and clear her head, she heard a muffled wail. Two seats down, Miranda covered her mouth with a shaking hand and stared at her work, tears welling. Everybody pretended not to hear her or see her as she ran out. Elaine squinted at Miranda's bench, scanning the various solutions. She recognized all of them, and saw the cause of Miranda's distress. Miranda had not made one of the necessary mixing reagents. In the time it would take to make the reagent now, the rest of her work would degrade. She would have to start over with... three hours left. Her half hour head start had become a three hour penalty.

A few minutes later, Miranda returned to her bench with a startling expression of conviction, suddenly resilient despite her previous outburst and bleak odds.

Something about that look unnerved Elaine.

Finally, the last reaction finished and Elaine turned off her burner. She had ten minutes while that cooled before she could move on to the next step. She slipped out of the chemistry lab into a parlor, falling onto a small armchair and leaning against the backrest. The room was quiet, free from odorous chemicals and the thick air of stress. It was almost perfect, except that she was not alone.

"Carter," Tether said in greeting.

Elaine ignored him.

"Alright, you're not talking to me. Fair," he said. "How about a peace offering? You have the black reference book open to page 161." Her eyebrows raised. He truly never missed anything, did he? "I recommend looking at 247."

She narrowed her eyes at him. What game was he playing? When it became clear she wouldn't respond, Tether stood, heading back to the laboratory.

Page 247 of the black reference book, she thought once he was gone. Somehow, page 247 was a trap. Page 247 had information that would set her down the wrong path, she was sure of it. Page 247 was a trick. With Tether, everything was.

Though, as she thought about the part of the reaction that the latter half of the book covered, doubt crept in. Then a dreadful eureka forced her to bolt back to the lab. She had forgotten to add an aluminum catalyst to one of the reagents.

But when she returned to her bench, the aluminum catalyst was the least of her worries. Tether leaned over her station, pipet in hand. A pipet full of her solution.

"What are you doing?" she hissed.

Tether wasn't startled by her voice, nor did he appear fazed by the venom in it. He slowly set the pipet down and turned around. "Helping you." He watched her closely for a reaction.

She gritted her teeth at his calm demeanor. "You're screwing with my experiment," she corrected with a pointed glance at the vials behind him.

"No, I'm trying to help you," he insisted. His eyes were the ocean during a storm.

"Care to elaborate? Or are you going to keep treating me like an idiot?"

"I don't think you're an idiot." For a fraction of a second, his mask lifted, face expressing guilt and regret—two emotions with which Elaine was intimately familiar. His mask of apathy slid back into place before she could dwell on it.

"Yeah? Then would you care to explain this? I should report you." She gestured to his pipet.

He flexed his jaw in annoyance. "I saw someone switching your solution. I'm switching it back."

She rolled his accusation over in her head. "How do I know you're not lying? What if you're the one trying to take my solution?"

He rolled his eyes and leaned comfortably against her desk. "Now who's treating who like an idiot?" he quipped. "My work is solid, Carter. I have no reason to cheat."

"Fine—then who was it?" she bit out, still wary of his intentions. He feigned offense at her skepticism, so she said, "Given our history, forgive me for not being quick to trust you."

He hummed. "She was short. Maybe five foot one or so. Black hair, black eyes—that one, the girl over there." He subtly pointed to Miranda.

"You don't know her name?" Elaine interrupted, annoyed that he found this amusing. There were only forty-five of them left. How could he not know her name?

"I would've opened with that if I did."

She pursed her lips, then asked, "Even if Miranda did try to steal my solutions, why would you bother helping me?"

He smiled. "Consider it me atoning for 'our history.'"

Elaine's gaze darkened. There was too much to atone for. He had punished her for her kindness, caused her to struggle at the bottom of the rankings, always one mistake away from elimination, possibly from death. He was the reason Kate was gone. He was the kind of person to brag about hurting others.

Tether noticed the imperceptible shift. "What's wrong?"

She shrugged his question off, glancing at Miranda again. "I'm going to report her."

"Don't," he said quickly. Too quickly. "You'll regret it if you do. You were right, earlier, about not taking eliminations lightly. I'm not sure if they die. But... they probably do, and, although we can't do anything to stop it, we don't have to make it worse. If you report Miranda, it'll be your fault she's gone. Could you live with that?" He paused. "You're a good person, Elaine. You're the m—" he cut himself off. "Besides, she'll probably get eliminated all on her own. You won't even have to lift a finger."

He stepped toward her, his tentative concern catching her off guard.

"I have a brother," she said suddenly. "His name's Henry. He's only a year old." Her voice broke. "I don't want him to die."

The way he looked at her then, the pity... it was overwhelming, like a wave crashing over her head, sweeping her off her feet. A beat of silence passed. It yawned into a chasm, swallowing every wall she had built.

"I'm sorry," he said. Barely a whisper, but there it was. An apology she never expected to receive.

Tether swallowed heavily, waiting for a response. She finally looked at him, and her breath escaped in a weary sigh. "You didn't do anything wrong." In the end, he was just trying to protect his family as she was. He had simply figured out ruthlessness first.

"No," he said. "I shouldn't have tricked you into shooting your flare. You didn't deserve that. It was wrong of me."

She said nothing.

"Elaine?"

"Yeah?"

"Your brother won't die." Tether's voice was tender, but not with pity. There was something else between them now.

"How can you be sure?"

"He has you."

Wren read out the scores during class.

"The poison with the highest purity was formulated by Gino Gonzalez," she said to no one's surprise.

Ava placed second. Tether third.

"The fourth highest purity, Elaine Carter."

Wren didn't bother announcing the low scores. They were already gone by then.

CHAPTER 21

Tremors shook her hands as Elaine accepted the blindfold a servant held out to her. The fabric felt heavy now that she understood what came with it. A loss of sensation that trapped her in another dimension, one not governed by any physical laws. One that made her mind vulnerable to delusion, opened her ears to voices that wished her harm.

Still, the blindfold brushed her skin softly, as if its gentleness was an apology for what came next.

At once, her mind was ripped from her body. Black swam around her, depthless and unending, the sort of darkness that greeted a person after death. Elaine lost herself to it, sensation slipping away like sand falling through outstretched fingers. Within a moment, she was no one, nothing more than a wisp of smoke in the night.

And she liked being nothing. No body to contain her, no mind to torment her. No past to haunt her. Just weightlessness and boundless freedom.

Time meant little to an absent mind, and so she didn't count how much of it passed before the darkness shifted. Light pierced through the murky shadows, shapes becoming clear in the distance. Then she was thrust into her body, able to form thoughts again.

All around her a world constructed itself. Not her world. The buildings that shot up didn't belong to humanity; they were disk-like in structure and floated in the sky, untethered to the ground.

One would think that a world would take time to grow, but this one did not. The sky appeared within seconds, a murky orange expanse, and the light of two suns glinted off a thousand floating metal domes.

Elaine was a viewer then at once a participant, watching the world piece itself together from the outside and then standing inside one of the metal structures.

She found herself staring into a mirror. Yellow eyes stared back. A yelp twisted in her throat as she beheld her body—the body that was not hers but she now occupied. She had the strangest features: skin the color of stone, hair the texture of copper wires and the appearance of spun silver. Still, the body was distinctly humanoid. Two legs, two arms, a neck, and a head.

"Heisa," said a voice. Elaine spun around to face a man with the same ashen skin and silver hair. "The dignitaries are waiting." His mouth framed words, but the motions didn't match what Elaine heard. He spoke in some other language, and her brain translated of its own accord.

Elaine followed the man to a tube hugging the wall. Turquoise glass slid into the metal wall, and once they stepped inside it closed around them. There were no buttons to press. The tube shot down at a speed that made her hair float as a magnetic force held her down. Slowing to a stop, the lift released them into another room much like the one they had come from.

The three people waiting for them—the dignitaries, she assumed—greeted them by stomping their feet. The man beside her did the same, so Elaine copied the motion. They sat around a table that rose from the floor like a lily pad sprouting to the surface of the water.

"The clans cannot be allowed to act in this manner," said one of the three.

"We must send them a message. Warn them that they cannot continue," agreed another.

"You wish to deploy the yverns," said the man who had summoned her here. Somehow, she knew that this man was her friend, and that the other three were not. The dignitaries were allies, perhaps, but she could not trust them the way she trusted this man.

The conversation continued, rumbling forward in the strange lilt of these people. Elaine tried to listen. This was her test, after all. But an inner voice told her she was wrong. Her test was not to pay attention to these people. Her test was much worse.

The whisper grew louder, until it became a chant thrumming in her skull. No, *no, no,* it sang, afraid. No, *no, no, no.* Her breathing became stilted with dread.

"Teller Heisa?" One of the dignitaries repeated, catching her attention for a single moment before the chanting stole her away again.

No, no, no! She scanned the room. Four expressions confused by her alarm. Outside, the thick red smog was nothing out of the ordinary. *Survive,* the voice demanded, before the chant abruptly ended, leaving her head empty.

Then everything clicked. She recognized these flying metal saucers, this strange sky with its two suns. She'd seen it before—in that room hidden behind the stereogram. A terrible wave of apprehension overcame her as she remembered that this world was about to fall.

"Heisa?" the man, a friend to this woman, said, tone concerned.

"We have to run," Elaine implored. She could tell they understood her; a questioning fear slanted their features. "Something bad is about to happen."

Fire. Raging fires that would consume home after home, person after person. Purposeful fires to destroy this planet and everyone on it. The three dignitaries looked between themselves, clearly annoyed by her outburst.

Elaine grabbed the man's hand and tugged him toward the tube. "How do we get outside?"

She was relieved that he didn't waste time questioning her. "Here."

"What are you doing?" the most forward of the dignitaries asked.

The tinted glass began to close. "Something bad is going to happen," she warned again. "If you want to survive, I recommend getting out of here." Then she shot down the tunnel to the crystal planet floor.

"Heisa, I will follow orders, but I would like to know the reason for your alarm," the man said.

How could she explain that she wasn't Heisa, that she didn't belong to this planet, that this was just a memory, and that everyone here was already dead? "Just trust me," Elaine said instead.

Red sand flew into her mouth when the lift opened. She coughed and swallowed some of it.

"Now what?"

Now what? Survive—that was her test. And she had the advantage of knowing how the world would end. Burning buildings would crash into the land.

"Is there a cave nearby? Preferably one with water?"

The man thought about it for a worrisome moment before answering, "Yes, though the entrance would take half a day to reach by foot."

Elaine blanched. How long did they have? She didn't know, and with no other option, they began to trek through the desert. The wind was harsh and dry, stirring up a storm of sand. Her robes billowed angrily at the disturbance. No wonder these people lived in the sky. Anything constructed on the desert floor would erode within a few years.

They stopped to eat after a few hours of walking. Elaine's mouth felt much like the landscape looked: dry and gritty. The man pulled a flask out from the layers of his clothing, holding it out to her. The water—if that was what she drank—was gloriously cold. While she took greedy gulps, he opened a bag of dates.

"You're not Heisa, are you?" he said. Upon seeing the truth in her startled expression, he smiled sadly. "I could tell from the moment you regarded me as a stranger."

"I'm sorry," she said, as if this were somehow her fault, as if she were real and not a figment of this simulation.

His sigh was weary. "Who are you, then?"

Elaine struggled to conjure an explanation. "I am from another world. This is not my body. I... I am not really here."

He laughed then, a bitter noise. "So then I am not really here, either."

Elaine didn't know what to say to that.

"I am Tessen Heiran," he said. Before she could reply, he continued, "Do not tell me your name. I do not wish to know."

She wondered what she would do in his position—if a friend became a stranger, an alien who warned of extinction.

As they prepared to continue, the first fire started. The flame was so far away that it camouflaged with the sky, barely visible through the sandstorm. If it weren't for the rising smoke, Elaine never would have noticed. They ran. Even the sand seemed anxious, pummeling them, tearing at their skin. Elaine tried to shield her face with her hand, but it was futile. By the time they stumbled into the opening of the cave, her eyes watered and her skin was tender.

It was cold, dark, and quiet as they watched everything fall apart. Fires melted the metal homes, which fell out of the sky one by one, hurtling into the sand. She heard faint screaming.

Then her vision faded to black.

CHAPTER 22

It was one thing to fear extinction. It was an entirely other thing to witness it. And to live through five worlds ending, as Elaine had, changed a person.

The test was to survive, but Elaine understood that she never truly succeeded. The simulation ended before she could meet her end. In the first world, she would have eventually starved under the sand. And in the second, third, fourth, and fifth worlds, she had only survived the first wave of violence: a flood, an earthquake, poisoned air.

If the Fall were behind these massacres, as Elaine suspected they were, then they would have killed her in the next wave. Not a soul would have survived.

Elaine had gotten lucky when she discovered those videos. She was able to predict each catastrophe, giving herself a headstart in avoiding it. Yet that luck forced her to watch grand societies crumble. Each time, the part of her that belonged to that dying civilization crumbled too.

By the sixth world, Elaine was tired. She supposed watching planets be decimated and species go extinct did that to a person.

Her eyes opened to the inside of a cottage. If this were her first time, she might have mistook this place for her own planet. A cobblestone road outside the window gave her pause. She didn't remember this from the videos.

A woman opened a door falling off its hinges. "Farah," she said with expectation. Another life, another name.

Elaine followed the large woman to a cramped living room. "Take these to your father. He's in the usual stall," she instructed, gesturing to a crate of flowers sitting on the low table.

She obeyed, mostly because she didn't want to deal with the woman's ire, grabbing the crate and rushing out the door. The breeze carried the stench of sea and sweat. She followed the throng of people to the market. Colorful stalls lined the busy road. Vendors shouted about their low prices or the luxurious quality of their goods. One even had the gall to grab Elaine's sleeve and shove a roll of fabric in her face. "Fine silk. Imported all the way from Inam," he proclaimed.

Some woman challenged his claim and Elaine seized his momentary distraction to spin out of his grasp. All around her people clamored. This was by far the most lively world she had entered.

"Do you believe the rumors about a treaty?" someone asked.

"Verali save the new emperor," said another.

"Farah!"

She spun around. A man waved her over from behind a wall of bright flowers. The smile on his face made her briefly happy, before she realized this man was most certainly dead now.

"Here," he said, taking the box from her and setting it on the floor. Elaine joined him under the blue canopy covering their stall. "We've been busy because of the coronation."

She forced a smile at his excitement. Farah would be happy to hear that. How wonderful that they sold their flowers, ignorant of their demise.

"Clear the streets!" Soldiers shoved people off the road. "Clear the streets!"

Worry toiled in her chest. Usually she recognized the world by now. Hooves clomped against cobblestone. The flower man—Farah's father—rushed to secure his goods as a large carriage rolled by. As she helped him, she caught sight of the seal on the carriage door. Her breath caught. The gold swords, crossed as though in battle, sparked a memory of death: a woman falling off her horse, an arrow in her back, a man with sorrowful eyes, a robed figure basking in the destruction. And bombs in the background.

With a start, Elaine realized *she* was the background. This town was the background. If she squinted, she could make out a large palace on the crest of a far-away hill where the video had taken place. It had been nighttime when the bombs started, right? Elaine thought she recalled a spattering of stars, a waxed moon hanging in the sky. The video hadn't shown planes or anything in the sky to indicate where these bombs came from. How did one evade the explosions sent down by an invisible hand?

She hesitated before asking the flower vendor for his help. In the last world, authorities had chased after her for disturbing the peace when she forewarned of poison winds.

"What is it?" the man asked.

"Is there an underground bunker nearby?"

It was a miracle he even answered her with how perplexed he looked. "No. We can't dig down. Water's too close to the ground."

The sun began to slip. "Can we take a ship out to sea?" Perhaps the bombs wouldn't reach past the coastline.

"We don't have a ship, Farah." He said her name with a hint of suspicion now.

A finely dressed woman approached their stall, admiring the blue petals of some exotic flower. Elaine decided then that she needed to leave.

"Farah!" the man shouted after her, but his voice was swallowed by the market's din and her body vanished into the crowd.

Unfortunately, the simulation didn't grant her the memories of whoever's body it shoved her into. Farah would have known the way to the docks. Elaine, on the other hand, was about as capable of doing so as a headless chicken. Fortunately, the stench of salt and fish was foul enough to lead her to the water. After winding up in no less than three dark side streets, Elaine finally staggered onto the harborfront.

Docks branched into the sea like a maze. Ropes wrapped around sturdy poles, fastening ships to the landing. Lanterns swayed in the breeze. Sailors and traders walked over steep planks to board and disembark the vessels, some empty-handed and others balancing stacks of cargo.

"You seem lost, little girl." She spun around to face a tall, muscular woman in all black.

"Are you a sailor?" Elaine asked.

The woman paused to study Elaine's face curiously. "What's it to you? Are you a foreigner? No, your hair—"

"I need to leave. Now." The sea began to swallow the sun.

The woman narrowed her eyes at the urgency coloring Elaine's voice. "What's the rush?

"Do you have a ship or not?" Elaine pressed, annoyed by the delay.

"Yes. She's over there," the sailor said, waving an arm towards a modest sailboat close to where they stood. "Now. Why are you so rushed and how will you pay me?"

Elaine held back a string of curses. She hadn't thought of payment. Of course Farah had to be poor. Of course her pockets had to be woefully empty the one time she needed currency. She had no other choice than to tell this woman the truth and hope it was enough to convince her to take her out to sea. "Tonight, bombs will fall on the land. I'm trying to escape."

She could tell the sailor was a strange character, but Elaine hadn't expected her to *laugh*. Loud and brash, grating against Elaine's ears, the woman laughed until she finally said, "What are you, the next High Vera?" Elaine didn't miss the sarcasm, despite not understanding the insult.

She waited for the sailor's amusement to dry up. "Will you take me or not?"

A shark's smile. "Will you pay me or not?"

"I don't have any money," Elaine admitted. As the sailor started to turn away, she rushed to add, "But I can pay you another way. I'll work for you for a year, unpaid."

"Two years."

"Deal," Elaine said. What did she care? By sundown this world would be destroyed. By sunrise she'd be reborn into the body of some other doomed soul.

The earlier pack of people at the docks had thinned. Elaine followed her new captain to her boat. When they finally set off, night had set in. Elaine held her breath and stared at the sky. The stars twinkled and the moon spilled silver over the ebbs and flows of the tide.

"I'm Gina, by the way. So, how'd you hear about these bombs?" Gina leaned against the curved hull. She looked calm, still disbelieving Elaine's claim.

"You want the truth?" Elaine asked. Her truth tended to shatter people, if they bothered to understand it. Elaine doubted the sailor would bother.

Gina nodded, though the gravity in Elaine's tone seemed to have had some effect. She no longer smiled. Elaine began, "This has all happened before. There's this species called the Fall. They like to tear worlds apart. Yours is not the first world they've destroyed. They like to make a game out of it. They toy with their prey." These simulations had taught Elaine much about humanity's enemy, if they were rooted in fact. She believed they were. "They're coming here tonight."

Gina's scowl grooved lines into her young yet haggard skin. "That's quite the tale you've got there."

Elaine averted her gaze back to the sky, searching. "It is," she agreed quietly.

A while passed before the first bomb struck land. Maybe two hours or so as the waves rocked their boat. Gina shot up, eyes wide. Seven more hit in quick succession. Soon there were fires.

"What in..." Gina said, mouth open like a fish, looking between the slaughter and Elaine. The gruff sailor stayed like that until her back slumped and the images finally sunk in as reality. Her world was dying.

"The war was going to end. There was finally going to be peace today," she mumbled to herself, but Elaine heard. Perhaps after five rounds of this she should have lost an emotional response to the destruction. Yet a bottomless grief filled her chest.

Elaine wondered if the Fall chose their timing for this world on purpose, and concluded they almost certainly had. Was there anything more powerful than crushing the hope for a better world?

She waited for her vision to go black, to either shift into another world or awake back in her body. Neither of those things happened. A shadow fell over their boat.

By the time Elaine noticed the sleek bomb, it was too late. The missile crashed into them, tearing both her and the boat to shreds before exploding.

CHAPTER 23

Elaine ripped the blindfold off her face as soon as she could feel her hands. No voice stopped her from returning to her body.

She breathed deeply, somewhat surprised to be alive. She could still see the bomb hovering over the boat, could still feel it crushing her body, tossing her limbs beneath irate waves into a watery grave.

But no, she was alive.

She slowly realized that everyone was staring at her. She studied their faces. They were watching her with expressions of astonishment, marveling at her. At the fact that she had remained catatonic for this long.

Elaine set the record of surviving five worlds. Ava came closest, having passed four. After that, a handful claimed three. Most had only reached the second before drowning in a flood.

"You did crazy," Mason said to her during dinner.

She had been lucky to stumble upon the videos; lucky to live through so many genocides. *Lucky.* Elaine nodded absentmindedly.

"What's wrong?"

She set her fork down. "Nothing... just, I," she said, struggling to grasp her thoughts, loose threads flapping in a tornado of ignorance. "What were those? The videos—the simulations, were they actually of the Fall? Did those things actually happen? And how..." She shook her head. "How is any of this even possible?"

Of course, Mason didn't have the answer to that.

The trials perturbed Elaine on every level. The disappearances, the dramatics. But most of all, how none of it should be physically possible. Forced hallucinations, guns that could paralyze with an invisible shot. The truth behind it all was an unknown so vast that to ask a question was to fall deeper into the unending layers of mystery.

If those visions had been of the Fall... A chill settled over her.

"Why are you even here?" someone shrilled.

The entire room went quiet, heads turning toward the second table.

Miranda continued to scream despite the attention. "Some of our families actually need the protection!" Her eyes glinted feral, crazed like a cornered animal. "You're a spoiled brat, Beatrice, you know that?"

Her victim, a petite girl in overalls, clenched her jaw against the insults, then leveled back evenly, "It's not my fault you're not good enough."

Miranda's hand shot out. A sharp slap echoed. Beatrice lifted a hand to her red cheek, mouth open in disbelief. "Did you just hit me?"

No one breathed.

"You deserved it," Miranda finally said, though her voice wavered.

Beatrice stood. "Excuse me?"

Ava stepped in before a fight could break out. "Stop. You crossed a line, Miranda," Ava said, standing next to Beatrice. She towered over the two of them. "It's none of your business who here can afford to join a bunker or not. Everyone has a reason to be here. The National Bunker is the safest there is, and it's not your right to tell anyone where they belong." She paused. "My family's already in a bunker group, too. You want to know why I'm here?"

Miranda pressed her lips into a thin white line.

Ava went on, "I'm here because I believe in fighting for humanity. I believe in this war, I believe in defending Earth against the Fall, and I believe I can help. I'm not here for my family—I'm here for me. I'm here so that I can help protect our planet. And I don't care if you agree with my being here or not, but you do not," Ava lowered her voice, "get to hit somebody just because you're failing and you think you *deserve* this more. Because, you know what? You don't. You don't deserve anything. No one does. This is war, Miranda. What you want doesn't matter. What matters is that we have the best people fighting against the Fall." *And you are not the best*, went unspoken, but heard loudly by everyone nonetheless.

Miranda seethed, then spun on her heel and left.

The next morning, the ranks rearranged.

Elaine stared at the list while she scarfed down scrambled eggs and jam on toast. *Eighth.*

She had always considered eight a perfect number. Symmetrical across a horizontal or vertical axis, eight was aesthetically pleasing, and across cultures it carried the connotation of good luck.

And, for now, eight meant she was safe.

CHAPTER 24

For the sixth and final trial, they filed into the ballroom, sat on the floor and tied the blindfolds over their eyes. By now this was something of a routine.

Thrust into an inky blackness, a place devoid of substance, Elaine watched her surroundings take shape. Cement ground beneath her feet, a dozen or so shiny blurs that solidified into spaceships that gave away her location.

The spacecraft hangar dwarfed Elaine. It was a massive structure that seemed to stretch forever, with one opening to an equally massive launchpad. The hangar housed dozens of spaceships, from sleek, jet-like ones to larger, more bulbous vessels. Somehow she could tell how many people were intended for each just by looking at them; a perk of it all existing in her head, she supposed.

Except... when she spun around at the sound of a gasp, it occurred to her that perhaps this wasn't all in her head. Behind her stood the twenty-four other competitors—and they all squinted in confusion at one another.

Before they could attempt to sort out the strangeness of this shared reality, alarms went off. Red lights flashed overhead and angry blares yelled at them to move. Everyone scrambled to their positions—which they knew instinctively—and the machines powered on. Electronic whirring filled the space.

Elaine sprinted to a lofty ship, the one that called to her, climbing up the lowered stairs held by metal lines to the entrance. Ava was already in the main control cabin by the time Elaine arrived. Tether followed seconds later. Ava pressed different buttons in quick succession, preparing for takeoff. A beep warned them that the door was closing. Once the smaller ships had left, Ava flipped a switch. As their ship rumbled toward the launchpad, they strapped themselves into the three seats pressed against the wall.

Elaine studied her surroundings, wondering if these were the same ships they would use in real life to fight the Fall. Probably. Why else practice in them?

Buffed metal reflected the light that entered through the long horizontal window above the control panel. An army of brightly colored buttons and switches covered the board. In the center of the room stood a lonely table. Being assigned to this ship meant that they would stay at the back lines.

"We're an interesting group, don't you think?" Ava commented innocently, picking invisible dirt from her nails.

Elaine read the silent message. Ava and Tether were the top ranks, and she wasn't. First, second, and eighth—an interesting combination indeed. Ava hadn't meant it in a cruel way. In all their interactions, Ava had always been kind to Elaine. She was simply a pragmatist who took note of every detail, especially those that didn't make sense.

And Elaine being here didn't make sense.

She noticed Tether watching her as the engines started firing. "I quite like this group," he said.

Elaine hid her smile.

It didn't matter why the groups were the way they were. All that mattered was completing the mission—surviving the battle. Because the sixth trial was a simulation of a battle against the Fall.

The ship shook, and they launched into space.

Elaine's heart hammered against her ribs as she was jerked in her seat, belt digging into her abdomen and the skin of her legs to keep her in place. She shut her eyes and focused on repelling the waves of nausea that threatened to expel the contents of her stomach. The ship eventually slowed to a stop, though by then Elaine swore her brain had turned to mush and her heart had burst. They rose from their seats to stand around the table. Elaine waved her hand through the air, and a holograph rippled to life—a three-dimensional rendering of the battlefield. Earth behind them, and rows of ships in front. And in the far distance, red dots crawling towards them, foreshadowing bloodshed.

"The Fall," Ava whispered, as though they hadn't been real until now. As though struggling through the trials—facing her greatest fear, captaining a losing team, starving in the forest and almost drowning, creating poison from scratch under a time constraint, witnessing the extinction of other species—had not meant anything until this moment. As though she was just now understanding what she fought against.

Tether touched a finger to the holographic ship on the far right, its outline lighting up upon contact. "Hammer-1, base, how do you copy?"

Beatrice answered over the intercoms, "Base, Hammer-1, loud and clear."

"What's your status?"

"Green across the board," she confirmed.

Tether repeated that conversation with the rest of the ships. The repetition would've grown annoying had there been more of them; it dawned on Elaine how few ships they were manning. How few soldiers they were, even before the final elimination.

"We're going to have more people when the war actually comes, right?" Elaine whispered to Ava.

"We better," she said.

Tether's finger moved to a thinner ship. Across the armada, there were only five of its kind. "Shadow-1, base, how do you copy?"

Mason answered. "Base, Shadow-1, loud and clear."

"What's your status?"

"Green across the board."

"Cloaking is functional?" Tether asked, a question that only applied to these smaller "Shadow" ships. Intuitively, Elaine understood that cloaking would allow those ships to evade detection.

"Cloaking is functional," Mason and each person after him said.

"Two hours till the Fall get here," Ava said, pulling up a holographic timer. "What's our plan?"

A minute and twenty-one seconds of silence ticked by. Elaine's eyes moved from the clock to the chart as she said, "What do you think about trying to circle them?"

Ava gave the idea thought before nodding. "That could work."

Elaine looked to Tether. Hesitation flickered in his pause. Finally, he said, "Let's try it." She wanted to press him for his thoughts. Clearly, he had his doubts about the plan. But he turned away before she could ask, leaving to man one of the ships' armaments.

Ava relayed the plan to all the ships via the holographic communication system. Elaine glanced at the time. One hour and forty-six minutes for the selected ships to maneuver to the proper coordinates.

One hour and forty-six minutes until the enemy they had been waiting for for the past year finally arrived. Elaine had to remind herself that none of this was real. That whatever happened during this battle, the death that would ensue—it wasn't permanent. Still, her fingers twitched with anxiety.

"Can you go check the inertial dampeners?" Ava twisted around from the control panel to glance at Elaine. "I'm getting an alert—I don't think it's serious, but could you check just in case?"

"Sure," Elaine said, tearing her eyes from the chart, away from the ever-nearing red splotches of death.

Like everything else about this trial, the inside of the ship was both familiar and foreign, new and not. It almost gave her a headache, seeing something for the first time but also knowing it intimately. She knew the cramped hallways like the back of her hand, and found the inertial dampeners without much guessing. They were tucked in a closet no more than a couple square feet, barely enough space for all the vibrantly colored panels.

Elaine approached the malfunctioning panel. After removing the protective covering, she discovered that one of the fuse decouplers was blown. She retrieved a backup decoupler and replaced the damaged one, then made her way back to the main cabin. Down one of the halls she noticed Tether sitting in front of a domed window. He shifted, as if he could sense her gaze. Then he turned around to face her.

"Hey," she said dumbly.

Tether smiled, but it didn't reach his eyes. "Want to sit here for a minute?"

She nodded. Ava wouldn't miss her.

Elaine slid into the window, which was large and arched enough to cradle her. The glass felt cold, even through her clothes. When she looked down, her breath caught. Earth hovered below, curving into a vast darkness only broken by pinpricks of starlight. Earth, bright and blue and home—delicate and vulnerable and threatened.

"It's beautiful, isn't it?" she breathed.

"It is," he agreed, though he sounded more troubled than awed.

Elaine focused on him. Black curls fell over his forehead, and they shifted ever so slightly when he sighed. "What's wrong?" she asked, because it wasn't just the impending battle. The tension in his posture, in the faint lines between his brows—something more than the battle was bothering him. She had never seen him so fazed.

"Nothing," he said evenly, a master at burying emotions. "I just don't like our odds."

When have the odds ever been in our favor? There was something else, something more, but she didn't press him. Instead, she admitted, "I don't think I'm supposed to be here. I think there's been a mistake." *Here*, as in on the commanding ship, as in being someone with power.

"You are," he said, then noticed her fidgeting. "Nothing about any of this is an accident. Whoever's running the trials thinks you belong here, so you belong here." He sounded almost bitter, but not at her. She stopped trying to read into the subtleties of his current mood—it would only worsen her headache.

"Who do you think's in charge? The ghost-woman?" At his puzzled expression, she clarified, "Sorry—that's what I've been calling that older lady who's always drifting around and giving instructions. She looks like a ghost."

He was grinning, his previous disquiet forgotten. "You know she can probably hear you right now, right?" Elaine went red, and he continued, "No, I don't think it's her. She seems more like a messenger."

"She can probably hear you, too."

"I'm not the one who called her a ghost," he retorted, amusement alight in his eyes.

"I didn't mean it in a bad way," she said defensively, but smiled anyway.

A silent moment passed. They were both smiling through it, at each other. Slowly, the moment released them into something else, something sweeter. Her blood thrummed as his gaze turned heavy.

"Elaine!" Ava called, voice tearing through the halls and yanking her from the sweet silence.

"I should go," she said, and Tether nodded, though his gaze didn't leave her until she disappeared into another hall. She was flustered as she walked to the control room—flustered, all because he had looked at her with those eyes, all because of the unspoken words in that gaze.

People didn't change, but Tether had. Gone was the boy who would trick and cheat without remorse. She couldn't figure out what had caused the shift. More curious was that she couldn't tell if it was a good thing or not.

Ava narrowed her eyes at Elaine's flushed cheeks. "You fixed the dampeners," Ava stated more than asked. Elaine supposed the screen would have told Ava when she'd finished replacing the fuse decoupler. Which meant Ava had noted her absence as more than mechanical work.

"What's going on?" Elaine asked, shoving down her rampant thoughts.

"The last call came in. Everyone's in their positions. Does this look good?" Ava gestured to the chart.

Three ships on either side of where the first wave of three of the Fall army would greet them. One Shadow ship cloaked in the wings, prepared to circle around the back once the Fall were close enough. "Looks good."

Now they waited.

CHAPTER 25

The circle tactic failed, and miserably at that. The first cluster of Fall ships was a trap. The ships were not really ships at all, but bombs that obliterated the ten human vessels sent to circle them.

"Why don't we get exploding spaceships?" Ava had muttered angrily.

So began the battle—with a major loss. The biggest shame was losing a Shadow ship. Now they had a pitiable four of their most valuable weapons left.

Fortunately and unfortunately, the next wave of Fall ships were not bombs, but actual Fall-manned spacecrafts. Around ten of them arrived a half hour later and began shooting as soon as they were in range. Beams of light blasted from thin cannons, so strong they melted holes through the reinforced metal, effectively killing the damaged ship's inhabitants.

"Spread out!" Elaine said over the intercoms. "All shadows deploy cloaking until the attack is over!"

She worked with Ava to maneuver their ship, narrowly avoiding a laser that would've ripped them clean in half. "Tether, for God's sake, shoot them!" Ava shouted, flipping a switch that sent their engines into overdrive.

Two Fall ships tailed them, and for a tense moment, it seemed like they might be driven into Earth or blasted to pieces by a laser. "Tether!" Elaine cried, then heard a loud hum and saw metal hunks of the Fall ship floating by. Another hum, and the second enemy spacecraft blinked off the holographic map.

Out of nowhere, a black Fall ship dropped in front of them to the one spot Tether couldn't shoot at and aimed its laser straight at the control cabin.

"Help—" Elaine was in the middle of saying when an invisible shot took down the threat. Then a human ship materialized, cloaking falling away. With the preventative communication block removed, Elaine was able to see Mason on a screen projected on the glass.

"Thanks," she said, as her attention shifted between multiple data displays. He gave a thumbs up before his cloaking re-engaged and his feed disconnected.

Within the hour, half the Fall ships were defeated. It looked as though they might stand a chance. Then the third and final wave arrived. At least seven hundred black ships, some armed with weapons they hadn't even seen before, filled the dark expanse.

"Well, we're screwed," Elaine said after gawking. "This whole thing is rigged."

Tether joined them in the main cabin, since the Fall ships wouldn't arrive for another few hours. But he was quiet. They were going to lose. Elaine could feel it in the way her breathing calmed in finality. The odds weren't stacked against them—the odds were squishing them like a boot crushing an ant.

If they were going to lose no matter what they did, perhaps there was no point in trying to win—not in the conventional sense of the word, at least.

"We need to send Mason away," Elaine said, her thoughts colliding into one succinct, reckless idea.

Ava immediately protested. "Are you crazy? He's the last Shadow. We need to use him in our offensive."

Tether kept quiet, eyes fixed on Elaine as she said, "We both know an offensive won't work. They've got us too outnumbered and we'll lose the last ship that can cloak."

Ava took in a frustrated breath. "Same thing as sending him away, isn't it?"

"No, it's not," Tether said, finally understanding Elaine's last-ditch plan. "If he's gone, he lives."

Elaine nodded. "We're never going to win this. The best we can do is survive, even if that means keeping only one person alive."

So Elaine explained her plan to them, and once they had ironed out the trickier details, they relayed the message over the intercoms. Tether returned to his post, preparing the shot that would doom them all—especially if it worked.

Elaine drummed her fingers on the table while Ava went about making sure all the right buttons were pressed and the right switches were flipped. Their plan relied on two things: hydrogen and luck. While in the weapons room with Tether, Elaine had noticed a detail about one of their missiles. Its explosion used a chemical reaction that had hydrogen listed as the limiting reagent.

"They're here, Ava said tightly.

"It's not real," Elaine whispered to herself, before pressing a finger into the chart and ordering everyone to aim their weapons.

Once the Fall were close enough—dangerously close—and the last Shadow ship was far enough—perhaps safely far enough—Elaine sent up a prayer to whoever watched over the simulation and said with as much confidence as she could muster, "Now!"

"It's not real," she told herself again, shutting her eyes. Ignoring the fact that if it were real, she would be responsible for the death of every single person on the face of the planet. Lose the war to win the battle. Because this simulation had doomed them from the start, and the only semblance of winning they could muster would be to save one and sacrifice billions. A choice she—none of them—would have ever made had this been real.

Silence as they held their breaths. As whoever watched them from outside the simulation looked on in disbelief. As fifty missiles shot straight into the sun.

Elaine felt only the gentle caress of heat before her world went black, and only thought a single thought.

Supernova.

CHAPTER 26

Elaine usually hated change. She hated endings and grasping for a closure that always seemed to elude her. Change usually fractured her into a million irreconcilable pieces, then demanded she put herself back together again to move on.

The end of the trials was nothing like that.

Eliminations stole ten competitors from their beds in a final vanishing act, but nobody cared this time. They weren't sombered by the warning in the loss; they were freed by it. Breakfast tasted particularly delicious. Elaine felt lighter. Her muscles barely complained during training, even though Tom added an extra lap.

Their teachers, however, didn't act as though anything had changed.

When Gino strolled into class two minutes late, Kron gave him a hard look. "What was your take on *Team of Teams*, Mr. Gonzalez?"

Gino blinked. "I, uh, didn't do the reading.

"You didn't do the reading," Kron repeated. "And why is that?"

Gino shifted on his feet. "I wasn't feeling well."

"You weren't feeling well?"

"Yes, sir," Gino responded, though his confidence was quickly deteriorating.

"Then you should go to the nurse now and get better." Kron rose from his seat. "And you should hope she can fix whatever *sickness* you have." He said "sickness" with such condescension Gino shrunk back. "Because if you are incapable of completing the readings or showing up to class on time, you shouldn't be in charge of a single soldier. Don't think for a minute that I have any reservations about recommending your dismissal. Just because the trials are over doesn't mean the war is.

"Now go."

Gino hesitated until Kron pointed to the door.

Class proceeded on its normal course after that, all cheeriness leached from their brains like a poison drained.

The ghost-woman made an appearance at dinner. She wore a white dress that reached the floor, looking exactly like the nickname Elaine had bestowed her.

"Congratulations are in order," she said. Her face displayed no sign of celebration, but she continued on. "You have proven yourselves worthy of commanding armies. Tomorrow evening a banquet will be held in your honor. Attendance is mandatory. The banquet will begin at five and end at midnight. Clothing options will be delivered to your room after your meal."

Elaine lifted her eyebrows at the speech.

"A banquet?" Mason parroted. "Why on Earth are we having a *banquet*?"

"To raise our spirits," Ava said from a few seats down. "They ran us down with the trials. They have to give us some sort of reprieve before the real preparation starts."

Beatrice set her spoon down. "Who even is *they*? Who is that lady? She's never even told us her name."

Mason shrugged. "Who cares?"

Beatrice squinted at him. "I do. She's creepy."

Elaine was also curious about the ghost-woman's story. What in her past made her behave the way she did? What rank did she hold in the military to oversee the trials?

"Well, I don't know about you guys," Gino said, "but I'm excited about the banquet."

They all turned to him. "What? You like playing dress up?" Mason taunted.

Gino grinned. "Nah, I just figure they'll actually make the food edible for it." He waved the unseasoned chicken breast in the air. "What even is this? It tastes like pig sweat."

Mason roared with laughter. "Fair," he agreed.

When Elaine entered her bedroom that evening, three dresses had been laid across her bed. She studied them, running her fingers over the fabric. She appreciated that none of the dresses were overly grandiose.

One was a blush pink with an empirical waist, silk that shimmered iridescently in the light. The second

Elaine rejected immediately for its color; blue foreshadowed death, blue was the color of evil. She had avoided wearing it for a year now, and she wasn't keen on starting now.

The third would have stolen her breath if she'd beheld it as a child, back when she'd had a fondness for beautiful things. The dress had no seam along the waist, flowing freely to about knee-length. Gold glitter dusted the forest-green fabric at the bottom of the dress and along the edges of the sleeves.

She picked up the green dress with gentle hands and hung it in the closet, piling the other two on the couch in the sitting room.

A *banquet*, she mused, finally alone with her thoughts. How theatrical. For the millionth time, she wondered who had orchestrated the trials, who stood behind the ghost-woman and pulled the strings. Because everything that didn't add up, Elaine knew that person would have the answers to. And she had the sneaking suspicion that the answers might be worse than the mystery.

CHAPTER 27

The mirror decided to portray Elaine as beautiful the night of the banquet.

Elaine stared at her reflection. Her dark eyes were bright, not the depthless wells of loss they usually were. Her black hair hung to her shoulders, not the dull mop of knots it tended to curl into. Even the smallest details—the slight upturn of her mouth—made the girl in the mirror look like a stranger.

A stranger she had lost long ago, and who she wished she was more often.

The dress fit well, too; it hung loosely at her sides, glitter shimmering like a golden fire when she moved.

"You look amazing," Ava said when Elaine came up the staircase.

Elaine smiled shyly. "So do you." And it wasn't a lie: Ava's sharp features and feline eyes gave her an ethereal aura. She could've been a painter's muse.

They stood outside the ballroom until two servants opened the creaking doors. A long table in front of the windows displayed the night's meal. Gino had been right: the usual plain chicken paled in comparison to the array of soups, salads, meats and pastas filling the air with savory wafts of flavor. Light orchestral music played, though Elaine couldn't find its source.

The ghost-woman stepped onto a raised platform where a throne might have once sat. Her movement snuffed out the conversations. Then a man they had never seen before moved in front of her, poised to address them.

Mason came to stand next to Elaine. "Who is that?" he whispered.

She didn't know the man's name, but she recognized him. The man from the car, the man from the library. The man who never said a word but seemed to have many words to say. And before he spoke, Elaine knew this was the man with answers.

"Good evening, everyone. My name is Arthur Simova," he began with a charming, practiced smile. He looked both young and old, ambiguous in age like the ghost-woman. "Congratulations on passing the sixth trial. You have proved your worth. To lead armies against the Fall is no small feat. You will take up that task. You will bear the torch of hope. You will slay the giant." He paused to survey the meager crowd of fifteen. "However, if you are to succeed in this honorable endeavor, you must work together. For the seventh and final trial, you are to vote on who to keep, and who to cast out. Your ranks will be taken into account when reviewing the ballots."

His words rang out across the stunned silence. *Seventh and final trial.*

They stood frozen, staring at the stranger in control of their lives, staring at each other.

"I thought we were done with this shit," Mason said unamusedly under his breath.

They all had.

"Democracy is a lovely thing, isn't it?" the man remarked, as though talking to himself and not to the desperate crowd hanging on to his every word.

Elaine had the distinct impression that he was mocking them.

Servants burst from their places behind Arthur Simova and the ghost-woman, filtering through the crowd and shoving ballots into shaking hands.

Elaine glanced down at the paper, gaze trailing the dark cursive letters.

One person you believe should stay:

One person you believe should leave:

You may not vote for yourself. You may not leave a line blank. Please write neatly.

Sign your name here:

"You have until the end of the night to make your decision. The votes will be tallied before you leave," the ghost-woman said.

"Until then, enjoy yourselves!" Arthur announced, though no one reciprocated his excitement.

Elaine tucked the ballot into the pocket of her dress and tried to forget about it. She would fill it out later, away from prying eyes. The banquet transformed from a celebration into a political battleground. Easy conversations became masked opportunities to jostle for votes.

"This is stupid," Mason grumbled.

The ghost-woman and Arthur waited silently in the corner.

"Yeah," Elaine said, the ballot heavy in her pocket. "It is."

"I'm going to get a drink," he said. "You want anything?"

She shook her head, and he left towards the big jugs of punch and water. Before she could find herself standing awkwardly alone, Miranda tapped her shoulder.

"Hi Elaine," she said.

"Hi." Elaine glanced at Mason, wishing he would return.

"I'm going to vote for you to stay," Miranda declared, expectation in her tone.

Elaine lifted her eyebrows. "Oh, um... I'll vote for you, too," she said, because it seemed like the right response to make Miranda go away.

Miranda gave the fakest smile before flitting off.

"She said she was going to vote for you to stay, didn't she?" Ava asked with a laugh, coming to stand beside Elaine. Beatrice followed.

Mason returned with a glass of fruit punch. "What are we talking about?"

"How *Miranda* is going around promising to vote for everyone," Beatrice said. "We've heard her tell at least three people that so far."

Mason laughed. "Of course she is."

They watched Miranda approach Tether, who stood with Jace and Gino. She beckoned him to her. Tether leaned down to hear what she whispered. His gaze snapped up. He smiled at Elaine, eyes alight with amusement at Miranda's foolhardy ploy.

Elaine rolled her eyes with a barely concealed grin, turning away as Tether straightened.

"I wonder what she told him," Beatrice said sarcastically.

As the night wore on, the music grew louder and the tension ebbed. They chattered pleasantly, friends instead of competitors. When the clock struck ten, they were instructed to turn in their ballots. Elaine wound up at the end of the line, behind Tether.

He threw a glance over his shoulder. "Who'd you end up putting down?"

Elaine scoffed. "I'm not telling."

"Ask me who I put," he said.

She stared at him. His expression was open, like he truly did want to tell her. "No," she said.

"See, that's what I thought you'd say." He turned his attention back to the line. They moved quickly. In minutes, Tether was at the front. She would never admit to her curiosity, but she stole a glance at his card. A *person you believe should stay: Elaine Carter.* Her name, right there in his neat handwriting. As if he could feel her shock, he turned around.

He didn't say anything, but he didn't have to.

Less than a half hour later, the ghost-woman announced that the votes had been counted. A hush fell over the crowd.

"Miranda Hane."

Miranda looked as though she'd won the lottery before the ghost-woman continued, "Has received the most votes to leave."

Miranda's pinched face fell and she reeled back.

"Elaine Carter has received the most votes to stay."

Elaine froze at her name. It was like the moment Ava had chosen her first during the second trial. It didn't make sense. Why would anyone vote for her? She'd done nothing to deserve it. Ava should have won for her character, or Gino for his intelligence, or even Mason for his competence in the ring.

Not her.

"After ranks are taken into account, Miranda Hane has been eliminated." Which figured, since she was last rank and likely had only made it this far by cheating.

Everyone took in a collective breath. For a moment, they were still as a graveyard of statues. Wondering whether the ghost-woman would drag Miranda away right then, right before their eyes. Wondering if they would finally discover what happened to the eliminated. But the ghost-woman gave no indication she would remove Miranda from the banquet. Tears streaming down her face, Miranda ran out of the room on her own.

So Miranda would be stolen in her sleep as the others had been.

It was close to midnight when the first person started dancing. Elaine wondered if there was something in the music, some magic that made it deep and rich and moving and lovely in a way she had never heard before. They all joined in, converging to the center of the ballroom and swaying to the music, dancing like drunk fools. It was the most fun Elaine had had in ages.

Arthur took to the center of the dais at midnight's knell. The music stopped. He looked to Elaine like an actor walking onto his stage under a blazing spotlight. "Now, we understand that there have been some questions regarding certain aspects of the trials. Feats that you believe to be impossible."

Elaine stopped breathing. Answers, at long last.

"Humanity is on the brink of a war of the likes it has never seen before. Utter destruction. Extinction. It is not a war humanity can win."

"How inspiring," Beatrice commented under her breath,

"This is not a war humanity can win *alone*," he amended. "But you are the chosen ones, and this war will not erase you. You are not alone."

Elaine blinked at his words, trying to make sense of them.

"The Fall have conquered many peoples, reduced whole planets to dust—but no longer. It is time to put a stop to the senseless violence. And you, young humans, will do exactly that. So allow me to introduce myself again, with more frankness. My name is not Arthur Simova, though that is still what you shall know me as. I am not human." A surge of whispers blew through the ballroom at his declaration.

Not human. Then what was he?

"I am a Simovan, and so is my friend, your caretaker." He gestured to the ghost-woman. "We two are Simovan, and we are here to tell you that you are not alone. Simovous will aid in your war against the Fall."

"You are not alone," he repeated, and seemed to look directly at Elaine.

Aliens. Everybody had been in a frenzy about the Fall, but they hadn't even noticed what was right in front of them.

The foreigners had already arrived.

PART 2

THE FALL

CHAPTER 28

45,000 YEARS AGO

2,400 LIGHTYEARS FROM EARTH

When one's lifespan stretches infinitely, one unlearns emotions such as fear and elation. When one does not feel, one cannot live.

The paradox of eternal life had plagued Simovan society since the Crescent Wars, when the only other species of comparable might had gone extinct. Then came the first Ennui Passing. Shocking, for who expects death in a world wholly of life? And damning, for it meant Simovan society would unravel. Ennui would be their undoing—existence would be their undoing. How long until monotony drained the life from every Simovan and the last of them fell? A century, a millennium? Millions of years?

The first Ennui Passing changed the trajectory of Simovan history irrevocably. Augurs, despite the novelty of such an event, saw the end encroaching like a black hole. Ennui was marching them toward an event horizon that would snuff out all of Simovous.

It was a strange thing, to curse and crave existence. For eternity to mean death. Şef mused this in an empty room of the Acropolis. He ran his fingers over the canvas of a forbidden painting. Out of the hundreds made, only three survived, and all three were in Şef's possession. The others had been burned. The images were dangerous, too fanciful for the public. They depicted the first Passing as though it were a miracle. As though dying were pleasurable, something to be celebrated. As though it were brave to end life by your own hand.

Şef had given the order to destroy the paintings. He had seen a future of chaos and death in a world where they survived.

These three... Şef saw something in them that called to him. He couldn't explain what it was, exactly, just that viewing them lit an invisible fire within him. The artist had, quite sadly, participated in the Passings. Şef didn't lament often, but he wished the artist had survived so he could speak to her. Ask her what compelled her to paint these; if it might be the same thing that drove him to stare at them day after day, millennia after millennia.

"Şef," came a voice from outside the door.

Şef turned around, though he could feel the brush-borne child staring at him from behind.

"Come in."

Sprijin gently pushed open the crystal door. She glanced at the painting, disgust flashing in her amber eyes. There and gone before Şef could dwell on it. "The council is waiting."

Şef nodded, following his advisor to the council's meeting chambers.

"You should dispose of the paintings," Sprijin said carefully. "They are forbidden for a reason."

Şef glanced at her. Her hair glittered ceremoniously. She was one of the few who knew about his collection. "If my memory does not deceive me—" of course it didn't "—it was I who forbade them. These ones are harmless here. I can see it."

Sprijin said nothing. What could she, refute the Sight of the greatest augur Simovous had ever known?

The council watched their leader and his favorite advisor take their seats at the head of the table. They sat around the large table in silence until Şef commenced the meeting.

"We have found them," he said. Another species. The Fall's newest target. Finally.

The screen behind him flickered to life, its technology so advanced that the wall seemed to turn to glass. The jungle clearing that appeared to be directly outside was, in reality, many lightyears away. Lush green vegetation and dark soil not unlike the forests across this planet's Tessier Sea. Roots slithered over the ground. The only peculiarity was the fly-infested sloth carcass in the center of the clearing.

Two short, muscular creatures ambled onto the screen, each using his two legs to walk and holding a rock in one hand. *Neanderthals*, though none of the other council members would know this. Just Şef and Sprijin.

The two neanderthals grunted in an attempt to communicate, approaching the sloth, but they clearly couldn't understand each other. Şef almost pitied them. Within a few minutes of reaching their meal, the neanderthals spun around at twigs snapping. Three lithe humans burst out of the underbrush, one wielding a long stick like a bat. Even with their superior height, the humans didn't stand a chance. The neanderthals overpowered them quickly.

The one human survivor leaped away from the scuffle when it was clear he and his brethren had lost, sprinting into the jungle, blood dripping from his arms and chest from bite marks and gashes.

Watching the humans was like staring at a reflection, if the mirror was blurry and stole brain cells. They had the same bone structure as Simovans, and even their faces looked similar.

Coincidences didn't exist under the laws of the universe.

The humans were too primitive to engage with yet. But Şef had waited this long already. What was another forty thousand years? Another drop in the endless bucket of eternity.

Şef focused on the screen. The two neanderthals tore into the sloth with their hands and rocks. They enjoyed their meal, hardly noticing as shadowed figures gathered among the trees. Only once the humans spoke, with much gesticulation and variance of tone, did the neanderthals turn around.

This time, the neanderthals stood no chance. Not against the superior communication of Homo sapiens. Six humans surrounded the neanderthals, three forming a close circle, and three farther back, still shrouded by jungle. One hooted, and not a heartbeat passed between that sound and an onslaught of rocks. Enough of the stones struck true, leaving the neanderthals bloodied and angry. The rocks stopped raining as the closer circle of humans tightened, drawing nearer with their bats raised.

Soon two more carcasses littered the jungle floor.

A seventh human emerged from between the trees, beating a hand on his chest victoriously. His blood glistened in the sunlight. Knocking around a few neanderthals made the humans giddy triumphant. They thought they had conquered their greatest foe.

If only they knew what lay in store for their descendants.

CHAPTER 29

PRESENT DAY
EARTH

Life in Prysnen remained much the same after the banquet. The shock of discovering the truth behind the trials—the existence of Simovans—was washed away in the raging storm of strangeness that had been upon them since that first telescope spotted the Fall amongst the stars. Training continued in the early mornings. Breakfast, lunch, and dinner ran at the same times, and servants delivered the same hopelessly plain food they always had. Classes hadn't disappeared either, even though they would be gone by summer. Off to their deaths, to fight for hope and the slimmest of chances that humanity might survive the Fall.

Though there were some changes. Their lessons morphed into preparations for battle—schematics of ships, the different weapons in their arsenal, various formations they should make depending on the situation, and other critical life-or-death concepts.

In the evening, they went up to the fifth floor to practice in simulations. Day after day, they slipped on blindfolds and were transported to a starry battlefield—and they lost every time. In the first week, they shrugged off the losses, entering each simulated battle with renewed vigor. But by the end of the third week, their fatigue was apparent in the quiet tiredness with which they tied their blindfolds.

Elaine had resigned herself to the fact that she would most likely die, that she might never see Henry or Helen or Evan again. But what fueled her, what kept her devouring each lecture and fighting until her last breath in each simulation, was that faint glimmer of hope. Even if she died, their effort might allow the next waves of human battalions to succeed. And after everything, that didn't seem so terrible, trading one life for billions. For Henry's.

They began learning about their enemy on a chilly spring morning, tucked away in a quaint room on the third floor where Wren held her lectures.

"The Fall are pure evil, even in the most objective sense of the word," Wren began. The petite woman had taught them chemistry during the trials but had since transitioned to other subjects. "Though they are much like humans in stature." She pulled down one of those old-fashioned screens from the ceiling. It made a faint zipping noise as it descended, before stopping to reveal a skeletal illustration and anatomical diagram—exact matches to the ones from the chemistry trial. Elaine tilted her head at it. Had they developed poisons for the Fall?

"Although the chances are slim that you will ever engage in hand-to-hand combat with a Fall, they are not zero. So you should know how to defend yourselves."

Wren picked up a pencil from her desk and wielded it as a pointer. She pressed the eraser into the spot on the diagram where the Fall's heart would beat. "The Fall are stronger than us, but they can be slain in the same way humans can. Aim for the heart or vital organs. Decapitation works, too."

She paused to punctuate her next point. "Do not hesitate to kill a Fall. They, by their nature, will not hesitate to kill you. Don't let your humanity be the reason you die."

She pulled down the rendering of a brain; again the same as the one in the booklet. "Their brains are very different from ours. For one, they are intrinsically driven to destruction. Their psychology is hard-wired to crave slaughtering other species on the scale of extinction."

Gino raised his hand. "How come they don't just kill each other if they're so destructive?"

Wren concealed a smile, which meant she'd been expecting that question. "What do you think?"

Gino hesitated. In Wren's chemistry class, everyone had recognized him as the undisputed best. The formulas came to him naturally, the products and reactants playing as characters in his mind, he'd explained once. It seemed his gift did not extend to the psychology of monsters. "A charismatic leader," he answered finally, phrasing it as a question. "Like in cults."

Wren gave one of those half-nods, a slight bow of her head, to acknowledge that the response had some merit.

"Charismatic leaders have driven societies to commit terrible acts," Beatrice agreed.

"The Fall have been around for hundreds of thousands of years," prompted Wren. "And unlike the Simovans, they are not immortal. Their lifespans are roughly double ours." So they could not have been led by one charismatic leader throughout their entire murderous crusade.

Elaine's desk was at the edge of the room, pressed up against one of three tall windows that looked out at the gardens. She thought about how two species could be so alike, yet so different. Take humans and the Fall, for example: physically indistinguishable, yet one was bent on purging the universe, and the other simply... existed. For a brief moment, she wondered if their only difference was power. Humans had committed terrible atrocities, too, hadn't they?

But Elaine couldn't believe humanity could ever come close to the Fall's evil, not even with all the technology and might in the universe.

Or bees and ants, she mused—an example that didn't force her to question human morality. Bees could fly, and ants were stuck on land, but their societies mirrored each other—

Her brain lit up. "A hive mind," she exclaimed.

Wren nodded, a full swoop of her head now, and explained, "Their society operates on a very unique social structure. You could compare them to bees, if you'd like. The Fall have one leader, a queen, and through her they are linked to a hive mind, as Elaine said. That is what makes them so formidable—they are organized in a way we can only begin to understand.

"Today, we will be discussing the Fall's instincts. If you can understand their instincts, you can predict their behavior, especially in high-stress situations like battle," Wren said, tugging on the screen so that it disappeared.

"If you are to remember one thing about the Fall, let it be this: they will do whatever it takes to protect the hive. A Fall would sacrifice themself in a heartbeat, without an ounce of hesitation, if it meant a greater part of the hive would survive. A Fall is not an individual in the way humans are. They simply exist as a part of the whole. Self-preservation exists in the sense that they must live to serve the hive. But their self-preservation does not extend to saving themselves at the expense of the hive. Can anyone pose a situation in which we can use this sacrificial instinct to our advantage?"

Wren surveyed the room while her students contemplated the question.

Ava answered, "If somehow you threaten the queen without wasting many resources, or convince a group of Fall that there is a threat to the queen, you can lure them into a trap without actually needing to isolate the queen. Or, if you did want to find the queen, you could use a Fall's reaction as a sort of compass."

"Good. Now, the next crucial instinct is their reliance on the hive mind. They are connected through an intricate mental web to the queen. Their experiences are shared and collected into the queen. When she makes a decision, or feels a certain way, it is with the knowledge of every member of her species. That is how they are so incredibly advanced. Now, this is a strength, but it can also be a weakness. Can anybody tell me how?"

If they weren't individuals, and lived their entire lives as part of a system, perhaps losing that link would destroy them, make them deranged beyond function. "If you can separate a Fall from the source of the hive mind, the queen, they might go crazy," Elaine said. The image of the prisoner in the hospital gown flashed in Elaine's mind. "They are dependent on their connection to the queen. She supplies their thoughts, their feelings. But if you take that away, what are they then? Mindless husks?"

"Precisely," Wren said. "They are incapable of functioning on a high level when removed from the hive. Separating them is very difficult, however, as they are aware of this dependence. There are two ways you can disconnect them from the hive mind. One, cut out the part of their brain that links them to the hive. But if you are in a position to do that, you may as well just kill them. The other option is to separate them physically. In order to be effective, the distance must be great. At least ten lightyears."

"Wouldn't it be easier to just kill the queen?" Tether asked.

"No," Wren answered without hesitation. "There are backup queens. If the queen dies, or does a bad job, the hive will raise another queen to replace her." She paused, considering. "But if you did manage to kill the queen and also find and kill all of her replacements, then yes, that could work, too. It would be exceedingly difficult, however."

Then again, surviving the Fall in general would be exceedingly difficult.

CHAPTER 30

On her way to her next class, Elaine overheard someone speaking from behind the door of an unused room.

The ghost-woman's voice floated through the outline of the doorway, hushed and urgent. "...and a dance, Şef? What are we doing here—why are we celebrating? This is serious—"

"You think I don't understand that?" Elaine recognized Arthur's calm cadence.

"The Fall are getting stronger," the ghost-woman insisted. "If we do not stop them soon..."

"I know that, Sprijin," Arthur replied evenly. "But all will be well—I can see as much. The odds are tipped far in our favor. Our plan will progress without disturbance.

And as for the dance, we must provide hope, or else they will not fight to survive. We must show that there is joy in life—that life is worth living and defending—or else they might as well surrender now."

The ghost-woman stayed silent, a begrudging agreement. Elaine almost walked on, thinking the conversation over, but then the ghost-woman said, "What about the mole? If we don't find the Fall's spy soon, this will all be for naught."

Elaine froze. *Mole.*

There was a traitor.

There was someone who could ruin everything.

"Our only lead is gone," the ghost-woman continued. "How are we supposed to identify the spy now?"

There was a heavy pause that made Elaine's stomach sink. Arthur was usually so sure, so right, so unbothered. For him to hesitate, there had to be something terribly wrong. "I will go back and search downstairs. Perhaps we missed something. We will find them, of this I have no doubt. All will be well."

The gears in her head turned. Downstairs—the dungeon? Did that crazed girl in the hospital gown have anything to do with this? Before Elaine could give the question thought, footsteps approached the door. With speed forged from months worth of laps around the lawn, Elaine sprinted into another hall and waited, pressed flush against the wall, until the footsteps retreated.

In Battle Tactics, Elaine took a long, hard look at her classmates. She tried to pay attention to the various maneuvers and schematics, but her attention drifted back to the ghost-woman's words.

Mole. One of her classmates—one of her friends—was a traitor.

"Elaine?" Kron prompted. "What do you think?"

She swallowed, trying to figure out what he had asked. Something about isolating the enemy. "I... I missed the question. Sorry."

"What should you do if a Fall gets you alone?"

"Call for backup?"

Kron shook his head, disappointment written in the creases of his frown. "Assume everyone else has their own problems to deal with. Anyone else?"

Ava raised her hand. "You should lure the Fall as far away from the battle as you can until they give up chase. They are only willing to go so far from the hive."

The rest of the day flew by. Elaine flinched at every sound, avoided every gaze, and read into every word. She kept revisiting one conversation in particular.

"Can't we try to talk to the Fall? Negotiate with them or something?" Mason had asked Kron.

That upset the former general. "For the last time, the Fall are not kind. They are the purest form of evil you could ever encounter. They seek nothing less than complete destruction. Do you know how many worlds they have destroyed?"

"No, sir," Mason said.

"Thousands. Thousands of planets, reduced to dust. Hundreds of thousands of societies, each wiped out in the blink of an eye. Trillions upon trillions of lives lost. Don't you think that, somewhere in those numbers, someone tried to reason with them? Do you think that we are special?" Kron held the class's attention with his steadily rising voice. He wasn't angry. He was scared. "The Fall cannot be reasoned with. The Fall destroy—it is all they know. Do not, for one moment, think that we are the exception."

He paused to weigh his words. "That's the problem with giants. We like to think that we're indestructible. We like to think that we can overcome anything. But we can't. Even giants can fall."

When Elaine thought back to that conversation, she focused not on Kron's speech or his fear, but on Mason's question. For a boy so driven to conflict, so quick to fight, she found it odd he would ask such a thing.

Dark clouds settled over the mountain that night. They conquered the sky, engulfing the stars and devouring even the darkness. Elaine was perched on the cushions of her windowsill, staring through glass at the iron gates that had once seemed so formidable, protecting a stronghold that had once seemed impenetrable. Now she knew better. Just as fog could slip through the metal bars and into their fortress, so too could the Fall.

The mole, the ghost-woman's voice whispered, replaying over and over in Elaine's head. She locked her door that night. Even then, she had trouble sleeping. Her mind buzzed with questions. Impossible questions that would drive her mad chasing for answers.

What did the prisoner have to do with anything? The girl wore a hospital gown—was she sick? The girl had deranged eyes, a deranged scream, and mental claws that pierced Elaine's brain—was she the same voice from that first trial? No. What did she want from Elaine? The girl was trapped behind bars—was she dangerous? Yes. Could she be a Fall? Who had put her there—Arthur or the ghost-woman or someone else?

Why was the ghost-woman arguing with Arthur? She had said the Fall were getting stronger—but hadn't the Fall always been strong? This wasn't the first time the Fall had struck, nor even the hundredth or thousandth. So why had the ghost-woman—or Sprijin, or whoever she was—acted as though this time was any different? Arthur had spoken assuredly—how could anyone be sure of anything in a game this deadly?

Who was the mole? They all had something to lose if the Fall won, a loved one who would suffer, that was why they were here—so what motive could anyone have to spy, to betray humankind? And they'd been locked in this castle for months with the Simovans—how had the Fall even managed to come in contact with any of them?

Her head spun. She pressed a hand to her forehead and climbed into bed as exhaustion weighed her eyelids down. Tomorrow she would try to figure everything out. For now, she needed rest.

Sleep deigned to visit Elaine for a few hours, before wakefulness abruptly yanked her from whatever nightmare she occupied and shoved her back into her body. Sweat clung to her skin and to the sheets, which at once felt stifling and unbearably hot. She threw off the covers, sharply inhaling when the cold air washed over her.

No clouds marred the sky. Sometime during the night they had fled, leaving behind dim stars and a half-dark expanse. Elaine stared out the window, her eyes glazed with fatigue. She stood by the frosted glass, too tired to be properly awake but too on edge to fall asleep. The lamps under the porte-cochère flickered, casting shadows that danced like the dead. And farther, where the treeline stood like a line of pointed teeth, ghosts shifted beneath the canopy. In her delirium of not being fully awake, Elaine swore she could see the missing children wandering the forest.

She shook her head, loose strands falling to the sides of her face. Standing here was useless. She needed to sleep—and if she couldn't do that, she could at least try to unravel Prysnen's mysteries in the meantime. So she changed into her training garb, black leggings and a black long-sleeve shirt—which also happened to make her nearly invisible in the darkened halls—and snuck downstairs to the library.

Elaine had always noticed how eerily quiet the castle was. But she had never been out this late and this alone. The castle itself was actually quite loud. Every creak had her spinning around. Every rustle of fabric from phantom drafts had her heart pounding. Every time a candle's flame jumped too suddenly, as though someone other than her had walked past, she suppressed a scream. She almost turned back more than once.

The library door was ajar, and she slipped through without making a sound. The moon reached its silvery fingers through the windows, draping the empty oak desks and gilded bookshelves in a faint light. Elaine marveled at the beauty. For a moment, there were no ghosts, no sinister noises, no dungeons, no traitors—only the ethereal vision of a venerable library.

She ignored the tangled feeling in her chest warning her to turn back. If she didn't figure out the traitor's identity, all their careful planning, months spent training, would mean nothing. They'd all be dead. The Fall would win.

So she pushed past her unease.

With the utmost gentleness, Elaine swung open the bookshelf. Shadows swam in the arched entrance. The passageway beckoned her forward with a frigid hand.

The dungeon was here, the door was open, and yet— she felt nothing. No thrum filled her veins, her heart didn't sing, and her skin wasn't prickling with an invisible electric current. There was only emptiness where the chaotic sensations should have been.

Elaine decided not to dwell on that emptiness, instead wandering into the darkness.

It was chilly. By the time she reached the spiraling stairs she was shivering. The temperature dropped precariously as she descended, the sort of cold that touched a person's insides. Her breath became mist and goosebumps sprouted along her arms. Her footsteps echoed in the cavernous dungeon, rocks she couldn't see scattering at her feet. She walked toward the single occupied cell. She hadn't forgotten which it was, though there were other parts of that interaction she wished she could erase from her memory.

There the prisoner...was not. The cell was empty. The lock had been burned, and the cell door was hovering open.

Our only lead is gone, the ghost-woman had said. *Perhaps we missed something downstairs,* Arthur had responded.

And in that moment, two pieces clicked together in her mind, the puzzle that was the traitor becoming slightly clearer. The prisoner *was* the lead. That girl was somehow connected to the mole. Someone from the outside had freed her.

Elaine had thought she was the only one who knew about the dungeon. But she remembered seeing Mason loitering around the bookshelf the day after the banquet. He'd been startled to see her. She hadn't thought much of it at the time. Now she couldn't stop thinking about it.

CHAPTER 31

Elaine noticed two figures crossing the lawn through a tiny window in the stairwell as she climbed to the fifth floor for the simulation—Arthur and the ghost-woman, judging by the way she drifted at his side like an extension of his mind. They walked with purpose, as though in search of something. *The missing girl*, she thought.

Soon enough she was sitting on the ground tying the blindfold over her eyes. She was thrown into darkness, then transported to that hangar to battle against fake Fall. Sometimes their assignments changed. Usually Elaine occupied a ship with Ava and Tether; today she was alone.

They tried to win.

They lost again.

But they had come closer to victory, their lessons finally paying off. And they would try to win again next time.

Black tendrils whirled in her periphery, languidly filling her vision until they were all she could see, all she could feel. A pure darkness that consumed every fiber of her being. And for those precious moments, she was nothing—she was free. She existed fleetingly in the space between simulation and reality, a space in which she didn't really exist at all.

This darkness had become familiar, after months of simulations every evening. Somewhere along the line, she had abandoned her fear of this in-between and begun to crave it. She had almost forgotten about the very thing that had made her afraid in the first place.

But, as most terrible things tended to, that thing returned.

Invisible claws wrested her from her ascent to consciousness. Even without a body to hurt, pain shot through her like a flare in the sky, bright and burning and unrelenting. She screamed, but made no sound. She thrashed against its hold, but did not move. She fought, but had nothing to fight with.

It caged her in darkness—darkness that no longer felt comforting or free—and studied her. She could feel its invisible eyes staring straight through her soul. It waited for a trepidatious heartbeat before addressing her. *We meet again,* it said, referencing their last conversation.

Elaine shivered without a body to shiver with. The voice ran through her, terrible and powerful—and also not as discordant as before. It still rasped, but not in the ringing, grinding way that had torn at her the last time it visited. It sounded almost human-like now.

Who are you? The question caressed her, as close to gentle as this voice could get.

She couldn't reply, though she desperately wanted to. She wanted to roar at this thing, to beg it to leave her alone. But she didn't have a mouth, vocal cords, or any other way to communicate.

Don't be so naive, it chastised. She jolted, realizing that it could hear her thoughts. *Of course you can communicate here.*

Here in her own mind, where this creature seemed to hold more power than she did.

It was entertaining her, as though it *wanted* to hear her speak. So she tried to, at least to delay it long enough so she could be rescued—if whatever had rescued her last time would even come back again—carefully forming words in her mind, then pushing. She pushed the thought with all her might, then heard the words reverberating in her skull.

What are you? she asked. The words had no tone or sound, but rang out nonetheless.

She could feel it smiling slightly. *Good,* was all it said.

What do you want with me? she tried instead, desperate now.

I want to know who you are, it answered simply. The same thing it had wanted all those months ago, since the very first trial. *Tell me your name.*

No. She couldn't. Somehow she knew that. So she didn't tell it her name, didn't even allow herself to think a single letter in it.

Then it laughed, and Elaine swore she sensed sadness in that sound before it moved. Quick as a snake, it tore through the darkness and reached for her memories. She cried out, and she knew it heard, because for the barest of seconds it paused. Hesitated. But it didn't stop, soon shifting through the pieces of her life. All the moments that made her who she was, all the times she had been hurt or hurt another, all the love she had given or received or lost, every success and every failure—*everything*—was laid bare to be scrutinized.

Stop, she begged, because she was in pain. *Stop*, she wailed, because it was getting close. *Stop—*

But it was too late. She could feel it find her, unraveling her final wall like it was nothing more than a sheet of paper on a husk.

...Elaine.

Disbelief and understanding wrapped up horribly into a single word. A question and a declaration, as though it didn't wish it to be true but knew it must be. It said her name the way a person said the name of a long-dead lover, finally accepting their grief and reciting it one last time as an act of closure.

Then it was gone before she could process anything, and she was sent hurtling back into her body.

Elaine was shaking. Her eyes fluttered as tremors wracked her body. She could hear distant shouting and fainter noises of concern. She could see faces, though they were nothing more than blurred streaks of color. She could taste the air, her mouth frozen in a cry for help. But she couldn't *feel* anything. Part of her was still trapped in that in-between.

The others swarmed around her, their distress palpable. A dozen bodies hovered over her, faces twisted in concern so raw it may as well have been them writhing on the floor.

"Some help!"

"Elaine!"

"She's not dying, is she?" someone whispered.

"Don't say that," another hissed. *Ava.*

The nurse burst through the door, led by Mason. The crowd parted to let her through. She crouched beside Elaine's head. But by then the tremors had subsided and Elaine lay still on the floor, staring up at the glittering chandelier blankly.

The nurse pressed a finger to Elaine's neck to feel for a pulse. Then she scanned Elaine's body for any visible injuries. Finding none, she tried speaking to Elaine. "Can you hear me?"

Yes, Elaine wanted to say. *I can hear you.* But her mouth wouldn't move. The assurance was trapped in her brain. And when she tried to nod, her muscles refused to comply. Before she could panic, she felt it: a push. A tender nudge propelling forward that part of herself that lagged behind in the in-between. Completing her.

Elaine gasped and sat up, coughing. "Yes," she exclaimed. At the sound of her voice, the crowd surrounding her let out a collective sigh.

The nurse's tight expression melted into one of relief. "Get some rest," she said, or something along those lines; Elaine was too shocked to pay close attention.

The next day, Elaine ignored the many prodding stares she received. Tom had added yet another lap to their run. She finished on shaking legs.

"Are you alright?"

She turned around. Tether stood a few feet away, regarding her in the same way everyone else was: like she was fragile. They treated her with the suspicion that she would break at any moment, speaking to her in low tones, careful not to make any sudden movements.

"I'm fine," she assured him.

"Do you have a history of seizures?" he asked, stepping closer while Tom drew the sparring ring.

"No... I don't know what that was. That's never happened to me before," she lied. The seizures hadn't, but the cause of them, being visited by that voice, had. Except this time, the voice had learned her name. Elaine didn't know what that meant, what the repercussions would be, but she had a feeling it was nothing good.

She walked around like she had a target on her back and couldn't quell the feeling that someone watched her while she slept.

CHAPTER 32

The forest wasn't evil, Elaine decided. Not as evil as whatever haunted the castle.

The forest was trees—wood and leaves—and soil—dirt and water—and wind—air and movement—and nothing else. Nothing sinister, whereas Prysnen was dungeons and prisoners and voices and traitors. Nothing and no one within those stone walls were as they seemed. She couldn't trust her overseers, supposed saviors who kept more secrets than they told truths, and she couldn't trust her classmates, supposed friends who might trade battle plans to their enemy as easily as smile at her during lunch.

So here she was, shaded beneath winter-shredded trees, trudging through the snow-covered forest alone. Tall pines sheathed their green leaves under a layer of white. The sunlight bounced off the ground. Icicles hung from high branches. She moved slowly so she could admire the world. Besides training, Elaine hadn't been properly outside for weeks. She hadn't noticed the seasons change outside the dropping temperature.

A bold squirrel darted across her path, clutching an acorn close to its chest. Elaine smiled at it, at the simplicity of the little creature's life. She envied its ignorance.

Sunlight filtered through the canopy, swaths of it gilding the forest. She stopped where the path broke through the last line of trees and opened into the lake. A rocky shore surrounded smooth ice. Elaine searched for the swan, but couldn't find it.

She drifted over to one of the larger rocks jutting over the lake and perched at its edge, hanging her legs over so that her feet hovered above the ice. Eyes closed, she took a deep breath. The fresh air felt nice, and the chilly surface of the rock against her ungloved hands did, too.

She lost track of time, sometimes with her eyes shut, sometimes wondering at the sky, sometimes gazing at her reflection in the ice. Elaine, as the lake portrayed her, was peaceful, the ice smoothing out the lines of tension and anxiety on her face and hiding the emptiness in her eyes. Perhaps not the most accurate depiction, but one that soothed her the same way seeing the squirrel had; it reminded her that there was beauty and innocence in the world worth protecting.

Though she could have spent the entirety of the afternoon here, Elaine lifted her legs, slipped on her gloves, and turned towards the castle. Lunch would be ending shortly and classes would commence soon after. She couldn't afford to miss a lesson about what order they should attack in and who should die first and how nefarious and superior the Fall were.

As she entered the forest, her foot landed on something soft and yielding, something not the hardened dirt she expected. She looked down and an anguished gasp escaped her throat. There, under the now-bloodied sole of her shoe, was the swan—lifeless. Her long, elegant neck was bent at an unnatural angle, and her black eyes stared lifelessly at the sky. Red streaks sullied her pristine white feathers.

Elaine had little time to mourn the bird's passing. A snap sounded. Then another, a terrifying break in the silence. Again, closer this time.

Despite her shock, Elaine had the good sense to run. Adrenaline kicked in, and she sprinted through the forest, away from the lake and whatever had killed the swan. An animal—a bear? But if an animal had taken the time to kill the swan, why leave it on the ground intact? Why not eat it?

Elaine's neck swung around at a distant woosh. Trees, she reassured herself. Trees were the only thing behind her. No bear, no—

Her gaze caught on something bright blue, stark against the muted colors of the forest. The blue flew forward, towards her, and her heart lurched out of its cage when she realized what was chasing her: the escaped prisoner. The crazed, animalistic husk of a girl with a murderous glower, eyes set on Elaine.

Elaine suppressed a scream and ran faster. Fear masked the burn of her muscles and stress of her racing heart. She couldn't think about why the girl was here; the word "run" hammered against her skull. *Run, run, run,* she had to run, she had to run faster, *faster, faster, faster.*

She spared a glance behind her once more, but this time saw nothing. Her vision swam. Green... brown... no blue of death in sight. Elaine still didn't stop, even as she wondered if she had hallucinated the whole thing. Or perhaps this was a nightmare, the culmination of her anxiety, and she would wake up soon. As her foot caught on something cold, she realized this was not a nightmare, and she would not wake up. She toppled onto earth, a rock scraping the skin of her elbow, and pain shocked her body—real, awake pain. She panted, breathless both from the chase and the fall. When she tried to move her leg, she found that her foot was stuck and her ankle hurt. She cursed, turning onto her side so she could free herself.

A dead body trapped her foot. Elaine screamed. Loudly. She couldn't help it. Her shrill brimmed with fear and disgust and horror. She had tripped on a dead body. There was a dead body in the woods. And worse, Elaine recognized it.

Before she could wonder how Miranda had met such a horrible fate, Elaine noticed a streak of blue. Her throat twisted in a soundless choke and her heartbeat filled her ears, an erratic gallop. Elaine shoved Miranda's torso off her swollen ankle, wincing as she stood.

She tried to move. She could barely walk without stars erupting across her vision, let alone run. All she could do was hobble forward on one leg and hope that the girl would find some other creature to torment. Though a quiet voice told her that was unlikely. The girl seemed to recognize her, visceral hatred flashing in her eyes when she beheld Elaine.

The girl finally appeared before Elaine, stopping a few feet away beside a crumbling stump. Her hospital gown was covered in dirt, and leaves adorned her knotted hair.

"What do you want?" Elaine's voice shook. She was careful not to draw attention to her hand slipping into her bag. She was careful to hide the cimeter knife behind her back. She'd stolen it from the kitchen. She would have rather been holding one of Tom's guns, but the knife was the best she could do without drawing suspicion.

The girl merely tilted her head at the question, more at the sound of it than to listen to the words, then stepped toward Elaine.

Elaine limped back, stealing a glance at where the manicured lawn peeked through the trees. If she could make it to the lawn, someone might notice her from the castle. Here, she was about as visible as a pearl at the bottom of a murky ocean.

The girl tapped a finger to her scalp. Elaine narrowed her eyes at the gesture.

"Stop," Elaine demanded, holding out a useless hand, keeping the knife behind her.

To her surprise, the girl did stop moving, angling her head as though listening for something. Elaine took the opportunity to escape, dashing as quickly as her sprained ankle would allow. The lawn inched closer. But she never reached it.

The girl slammed into Elaine's back, pinning her to the ground and snarling. Elaine cried out as her ankle exploded in searing agony and her face struck the ground. Still, she managed to stab the girl in her neck.

Sticky black blood oozed from the wound onto Elaine's palm and down her arm. The girl grunted as she removed the blade, tossing it aside. Like she didn't need it. Like it barely hurt her.

Elaine twisted onto her back in an attempt to throw the girl off of her. The escaped prisoner let out an annoyed growl. With a strength that did not match her small stature, the girl hit Elaine's abdomen. Elaine swore she could hear her bones splintering. Tears welled as she fought—futilely—against the girl's assault. None of her hits seemed to affect the girl, as if she couldn't feel pain. Elaine protected her face with her arms, using her good leg to knee the girl until she fell off.

Spars—the matches. Elaine had trained for this, nearly every morning for months. But she had never fought with a sprained ankle. She had never fought actually thinking she might die.

Elaine dodged the girl's fist, swerving horizontally then rising on her injured foot. As she prepared to stomp on the girl's middle, leg in the air, a pale hand reached out to her other knee, sending her teetering off balance. The girl picked up the knife before leaping onto her, and as Elaine stared into her eyes—dark orbs lacking any shred of humanity—she knew she was about to die. She could feel it in her bones.

She was about to become nothing more than a corpse atop dirt, waiting to join the earth. Perhaps someone would find her, perhaps they wouldn't. Perhaps everything she'd done for Henry would now be in vain. Perhaps Helen and Evan would hate her for failing. Perhaps she would finally see Lily again after all these years, finally get to tell her sister how sorry she was, how she had never wanted her to die, despite what she had felt; and perhaps her sister would say this was karma, to die alone in the woods as she had. Perhaps Elaine would be mourned, or perhaps the world would be too preoccupied battling extinction to pay her any grief.

Elaine closed her eyes.

Perhaps this was what her life had always been leaning toward, dying young and alone.

She waited for more pain to take her away. But the killing blow never came. Instead, the girl's weight was suddenly gone. Elaine's eyes flew open in time to watch her attacker's head collide with the sturdy trunk of a tree, ebony eyes fluttering shut. Elaine dared to hope they would never open again.

She turned to her savior, but "thank you" twisted around her tongue.

Tether was frozen, staring not at Elaine, nor at who he had just killed, but at his hands. He stared at his hands and said nothing.

"Tether," Elaine breathed, her ankle pulsing unbearably.

He finally seemed to notice her. "Elaine," he said, rushing to her side. He noticed her swollen ankle and took in a sharp breath. "Are you okay?"

"Is she dead?" she asked urgently with a glance at the girl's limp body. Black blood dripped from the girl's stab wound down the bark.

He hesitated. "I'm not sure. We should go."

He helped her stand, draping her arm over his shoulders and walking slowly so she wouldn't stress her ankle. They cleared the treeline and stepped onto the lawn.

"What happened? Why were you out here?" he asked.

She choked on her words, still disoriented. "It seems so stupid now... I was so stupid—I just wanted to get some fresh air. I should've realized..." It hurt to speak. Her torso was sore. "I'm so stupid."

"Elaine—"

"I was just going to let her kill me." She held back tears. "I couldn't fight her. I couldn't..."

Tether paused, letting her lean harder on him as she took in shuddering breaths, adrenaline wearing off.

"If you hadn't found me, I'd be dead," she whispered, more to herself than to him. She was foolish for wandering into the forest. She was weak for surrendering so easily.

"But you're not," he said gently. "You're safe now."

They started walking again. When they were halfway across the lawn, a crowd gathered at one of the windows on the second floor. Then two figures emerged from the garden hurrying to meet them.

The ghost-woman and Arthur had twin expressions of alarm at her state. "What happened?" Arthur demanded.

"The girl from the dungeon," Elaine said carefully, studying their expressions. The ghost-woman looked to Arthur, who narrowed his eyes at the part of the forest they had come from. "She attacked me."

"Where," Arthur said.

Elaine pointed at the path to the lake. "About ten feet into the forest." She paused, then added, "I think she might be dead."

"Dead?" the ghost-woman repeated, and Elaine couldn't tell if she was more relieved that Elaine was alive or upset that the other girl was dead. "How?"

Elaine glanced up at Tether and said, "I stabbed her in the neck and then Tether threw her against a tree. I think she bled out."

Arthur and the ghost-woman shared a look that held within it an entire conversation, then began walking to the forest.

"Take Elaine to the nurse," the ghost-woman said to Tether. "Fifth floor, across from the ballroom."

Tether nodded.

"Speak of this to no one," she added.

CHAPTER 33

Elaine thought dizzily that she must have hit her head quite hard, because her vision swam on the way upstairs and as soon as she sat down for the nurse to examine her ankle, she passed out.

When she came to, her head was pounding and, after a moment of confusion, she registered that she was alone. She vaguely remembered awaking in a daze earlier, seeing Tether in the chair next to her, him smiling and her mumbling something unintelligible before she lost consciousness again.

This time, she found herself on the pale blue examination table, thin paper sheet crinkling as she propped herself onto her arms. A slight woman with white hair entered the room, dressed in teal-colored scrubs.

"Hello, Elaine," she said, smiling warmly.

"Hi."

"Are you feeling better?" The nurse brought a wheeled stool over.

"Other than my ankle I feel fine," Elaine said.

The nurse started to purposefully push the tender skin around Elaine's ankle. "Tell me when it hurts."

When the examination finished, the nurse declared, "It appears you have severely sprained the ligaments under your fibula. Sit out at training tomorrow, or ask for modified exercises so that you don't put too much weight on your ankle."

She rolled her chair to a cabinet under the sink and retrieved a glass pill bottle that rattled as she handed it to Elaine. "You should take these to speed up the healing and numb the pain. It's Simovan medicine. Take two tonight and one tomorrow morning, and you'll be as good as new."

"Thank you." Curious, she asked, "What do you get for doing this?"

The nurse blinked at her dazedly. "I'm not sure I understand what you mean."

"For your job here. Are they paying you or something? The Simovans," she clarified. "Or do you get access to a bunker...?"

The nurse squinted at the air. "I..." she hesitated. Elaine read that pause; the nurse did not know why she was here. "I'm not—I'm not sure...I am here to help."

A startling clarity came upon the nurse, who repeated, "I am here to help." She continued to murmur those words like a mantra. Like a woman possessed.

Elaine took the pills and left without another word.

She could hear the nurse in her head as she descended the stairs. *I am here to help.* Over and over. An artificial purpose nestled so deeply in the woman's subconscious she couldn't understand her own choices. Elaine shook off her disgust. Had the nurse even chosen to come here? Had any of the servants? Had the Simovans asked permission before reducing the nurse to a function devoid of volition or identity?

She glanced at the amber pills in her hand. Simovan medicine, the nurse had said. After the same nurse had demonstrated her lack of mental control, Elaine decided not to trust the translucent ovals. Even if they could accelerate her healing, it wasn't worth the risk of losing her mind.

She shoved the glass bottle into the pocket of her jacket and turned down the hallway that led to the library.

The library was empty at this hour, save for one person who occupied the far corner of the room. Tether sat in a reading nook concealed behind a maze of shelves. He came here every day after class, and had since the beginning of the trials. And he was always alone.

"What are you doing here?" he asked when he saw her. He held a slight red book over his forearm.

"I realized I never thanked you. For saving me." *Thank you* was the least of it. She owed him her life.

"You don't need to," he said, setting his book on the low table beside his chair. "I would do it again in a heartbeat."

She stood awkwardly at the edge of the carpet. "Well, thank you anyway."

After a beat of silence in which he seemed to be contemplating something, Tether gestured to the other chair. "Would you like to join me?"

She nodded, toeing around the table and falling onto the cushions. She peered at the title of the red book. *The Sheep in Wolf's Clothing.*

"Why were you in the forest?" Elaine asked. She couldn't help but wonder why fate rescued her again and again while it abandoned people like Kate and Miranda.

Tether didn't seem surprised by the question. "I go there sometimes to clear my head. I was on my way to the lake when I heard you scream."

Elaine shuddered to remember her brush with death. She wished she could forget it, but knew she never would. Although that girl was most likely dead, she would live on in Elaine's nightmares. Her ebony eyes would haunt Elaine forever.

"I really thought I was about to die," she said. "I can't believe... I can't believe I just gave up."

"You're human," Tether said. "You froze. It happens."

No, she hadn't frozen. It had been a conscious choice. She had, for the sharpest of moments, accepted death. Welcomed it as her fate.

The door to the library opened. They both turned at the sound, where the ghost-woman drifted at the entrance calling Elaine's name.

Elaine smiled at Tether before leaving. "Thank you again."

He dipped his head, hiding a sad smile that Elaine wished she could understand. "Of course."

Elaine followed the ghost-woman to the highest floor of the castle. She still found Prysnen's warden off-putting, even considering her inhumanness. Compared to Arthur, she seemed lifeless. Worn, as though her eons of existence had eroded her spark of life. She regarded humans with little interest, despite Simovans claiming the title of humanity's saviors. Though that could be attributed to the fact that they would all die eventually, and she would not; immortality would make forming connections outside her species seem meaningless, Elaine supposed.

The fifth floor had a single hallway with two doors. One opened into the ballroom, and the other led into the medical wing. The ghost-woman stopped at neither of them. Instead, she continued along the hallway until she reached its end, a wall adorned with the portrait of some nobleman and his daughter. The daughter watched her father wistfully while he kept his eyes on the painter, uncaring.

Elaine's brows drew together as she wondered if the ghost-woman truly had gone mad after all. Then the ghost-woman lifted an impossibly pale hand to the etched bronze frame and Elaine understood. The portrait concealed a passageway. The ghost-woman slid a bony finger down the edge until it caught on a latch. The painting swung off the wall.

The ghost-woman gestured for Elaine to enter, though she gave no indication she would go in herself. Elaine obliged, shuffling into the passage.

Most times Elaine appreciated her height, but now, in the already cramped space, she lamented it. She barely fit through, her broad shoulders pressing against the sides of the tunnel, unable to crane her neck to see in front of her. She stared at her hands instead. And as soon as she thought it couldn't get any worse, the ghost-woman shut the painting and the tunnel was enveloped in darkness.

Elaine bit back a curse. She shouldn't have been surprised that the ghost-woman would close the entrance before she'd reached the other side. The warden had never demonstrated an affinity for gentleness with her charge.

Thankfully, the tunnel wasn't terribly long. She bumped into the exit within a minute and fumbled for the latch. Her fingers grasped a switch, and the wall opened.

Elaine fell as gracefully as she could—in other words, with absolutely no grace at all—into a well-furnished study. A midnight-blue carpet covered the marble floor. A sturdy oak desk stood before a large window embedded with misshapen bits of tinted glass. Elaine marveled at how the sun's rays would catch on the glass's color and cascade across the room in vibrant strokes.

It took her a moment to notice Arthur, who watched her from the corner, his hand lingering on the book he'd just pushed back into place.

"Elaine Carter," he said in greeting.

She stayed quiet while he took his seat in the leather chair behind his desk. He waved at the cushioned seat across from him; Elaine sat.

"You're wondering why I summoned you here," he said. She nodded. "I wanted to check up on you. After all, that must have been quite a traumatic thing to happen to a seventeen-year-old human child, no?"

She waited a beat before saying, "If I may ask... Who was that girl?" Elaine had her suspicions; Arthur Simova had the truth.

"A Fall," he said simply.

Elaine masked her surprise at his honesty. For a man so partial to theatrics and mysteries, he was very forthcoming.

"Why was she trapped in the dungeon? How long has she been down there?" If he was willing to tell the truth, then she had many more questions she wanted to put to rest.

"We held her there because we wanted to learn more about the Fall. They continue to advance. In order to remain ahead, we must understand their evolution," he explained. "She has been here as long as you have."

Elaine refrained from pointing out how reckless it was to keep a Fall locked up in a castle with human children. Instead, she asked the question that had hurt the most to wonder about. "You didn't... kill the ones who got eliminated, did you?"

His amber eyes narrowed in contemplation. "No," he said finally. "We did not kill anybody. We may not be human, Elaine, but we do have morals."

Part of her believed him.

But part of her understood that morals could be bent or tossed aside when inconvenient. War was usually inconvenient.

"Now, you must be going, Elaine Carter" Arthur said. "We will speak again soon."

CHAPTER 34

Elaine found herself going back to that little reading nook in the library evening after evening. One of those evenings, she was staring absentmindedly at a vase of roses that never wilted when Tether asked, "What are you thinking about?"

She rested her head in her hand "How I don't really know anything about you."

"Isn't that supposed to be a good thing?" He grinned. "Man of mystery and all?"

"Tell me something about yourself," she said. "Something nobody else knows."

He cocked his head. "A secret."

She nodded.

"Alright, I'll tell you a secret. But you have to tell me one in exchange." He laughed at her hesitation. "It's only fair."

Her secret, the one nobody else knew, was far too dark for this sort of conversation. "Fine," she agreed. She could tell him she was adopted, a fact most found interesting enough.

He seemed to contemplate what to say, as if he had many secrets to choose from. Or one terrible one.

"I was born in England," he began. "When I was six, my mom got a new job, so we moved to America. I didn't have many friends, so I wasn't sad to leave. But then once school started, I had a hard time talking to the other kids. My parents got worried that I couldn't form social connections, so they took me to see a therapist. Every Wednesday they would take me to his office, and every Wednesday he would try to make me normal. But that old man couldn't fix me.

"I started second grade at a new school because my parents thought it would be good for me to have a fresh start. But the kids were cruel. They found out about my condition and thought it would be a great idea to beat me up. Since I couldn't feel pain, they thought it would be fun to see what I would do." He shook his head, a leftover anger glinting in his eyes. "You know, we're learning about how evil the Fall are, but I think humans are just as bad."

Elaine didn't have anything to respond to that with. She wished she could disagree, find some argument that humanity was good and right and worth protecting. But kids had beaten Tether *for fun*. Humanity was capable of evil, too.

"They came to my house after school. My mom was going to come home from work soon, so I left the door unlocked. My dad was asleep upstairs and he didn't hear them come in. They found me on the couch and started hitting me. I couldn't feel it, but I knew what they were doing. I knew I was bleeding everywhere. I knew some of my bones were broken. I told them to stop, but they just kept going. They put a pillow over my mouth so I couldn't yell. I could barely breathe. I thought I was going to die."

His shoulders tensed, as though remembering the struggle.

"So I did—I did what I had to do. They would've come back again, I heard them talking about it. So I pretended to pass out. Then I attacked them from behind with a lamp. And I started kicking them." He avoided looking at her. "My dad came down and saw the mess. My mom got home, and they didn't know what to do because one of the neighbors called the police about the noise. There wasn't enough time to get rid of the glass or clean up the blood, so my parents came up with a plan to take the blame for me. They told me to tell the police that I passed out and when I woke up my dad was standing over the kids. My mom wiped my fingerprints from the lamp base and my dad put his on it instead.

"He went to jail. My mom was never herself after that," he said. "The trial lasted a year, and the whole time, they never told the truth. That their son was the one who did it. They loved me so much that he branded himself as a child beater and my mom lost her husband, all to save me. And you want to know the worst part?"

She didn't. She couldn't imagine it could get any worse than that.

"I never loved them, not really. I never cared that he was going to rot in a cell for my mistakes. I knew I was supposed to... I just never did." He let out a tense, shaking breath. "I wish I had loved them. I wish I could go back in time and tell the truth. I mean, it was self-defense, they were beating me up in my own house, and I was a kid; I'm sure my sentence wouldn't have been half as bad as my dad's."

Then he said, in a low voice, "The first time I ever felt remorse was when I did what I did to you in that trial. I've never felt bad about anything in my life before that. I'm numb physically, and I was numb emotionally. But ever since then, I... well, I can't explain it, but I care now. I *feel* now, you know?" A pause. "I think it's the whole world's ending thing. And now I want to tell my parents I'm sorry, I want to tell them that so badly, and that I love them, but I don't think I'll ever get the chance to."

He stopped talking. A minute passed, maybe two. His jaw feathered when she stayed silent.

"Tether..."

He finally brought his eyes to hers. He peered at her through hooded lashes as though trying to read her mind. Blue pools of sadness and guilt. He was drowning. And somewhere in those depths, she saw herself.

"I'm sorry," she whispered, unsure what to say, knowing sorry wasn't enough. "That's a terrible thing to happen."

He shut his eyes. "I didn't want to hurt them. I just wanted to scare them so that they'd leave me alone. But one of them got temporary amnesia, and the other one couldn't walk straight for a month."

It dawned on her why he'd chosen to tell her this story. A story that portrayed him in the darkest of lights.

"You're not a monster," she said gently.

The library was quiet. She could hear his breathing. She could almost hear his heart beating.

"You're not a monster, Tether. You were just a kid who didn't know how to protect yourself. You were alone and you were scared. You let your parents take care of the consequences because that's what kids do."

Elaine shifted on the cushions. "I'll tell you my secret, if you want."

He nodded quietly, the flash of curiosity like a lifeline pulling him from his past.

"My parents adopted me and my sister when I was six and she was four. We weren't biologically related, but it felt like we were. She was like my other half. We did everything together..." She told him about Lily, about their strange connection, the way they always loved each other but always hated each other at the same time. She told him about that day in the woods, and Lily's untimely death. And she told him about how happy she had felt.

Her deepest, darkest secret. A terrible, twisted truth she always believed would follow her to her grave. One she had never accepted. But now it was out in the world, set free, and she would have to face it.

She had wanted Lily to die.

Tether stared at her eyes like he was looking at her for the first time. Perhaps he saw himself in them the way she had seen herself in his. Tortured, haunted. Twin souls brimming with regrets. Yearning for redemption.

"You didn't do anything wrong," he said. "And I promise you, you didn't want her to die. Not truly, not in the way you think you did." He spoke so assuredly. "Sometimes you can't help the way you feel about something. Sometimes it's not up to you."

There was a hidden meaning to his words, like he wanted to say more but couldn't. But he sounded like he believed them. And in that moment, it was enough.

CHAPTER 35

As their deployment neared, melancholy thickened in the air. It became difficult to think past. Melancholy was like guilt, Elaine thought, an elusive beast without form, rearing on its haunches to rip your resolve to shreds. Impossible to hide from, impossible to slay.

One month out, Elaine had yet to fully come to terms with her fate. She avoided the trap of wondering whether she would live or die. She focused on her studies, memorized battle plans, and familiarized herself with the enemy through Simovan texts. If she would die, she would die for a noble cause. That was enough for her.

Yesterday, they had won a simulation. Spirits were high, hope rising and exploding like a dozen fireworks.

But hope was a fickle thing. Elaine didn't trust it. Hope coaxed a fool into a fighter.

But in calculated doses, hope was a powerful tool.

"I think the simulation was rigged," Elaine admitted to Tether.

He looked up from the physics assignment. "What makes you think that?"

"I overheard Arthur talking to that lady one time. He was saying something about how we had to hope in order to fight. I think they saw us giving up." She leaned against the sloped armrest.

He hummed as he mulled over her theory. "That's quite devious of them," he said finally. "Then again, we know nothing about them."

She could tell he wanted to say more.

"That Arthur guy says Simovans are here to save us, but who knows? Maybe they're the bad guys. Maybe the Fall aren't even real."

She considered telling him that the girl from the forest was a Fall, but said instead, "I don't think the Simovans are evil. If they wanted to hurt us, why bother introducing themselves? Why bother with the trials? They're giving us their technology, too."

Tether shrugged. "I guess."

They watched each other in silence. She noticed things about his face she couldn't believe she'd missed before. A small burn mark on his chin, a scar below his ear. Somehow, these only added to his beauty, making for a face worthy of hanging in a proud portrait. Elaine might have tried to paint him had she not been such an awful artist. She could never capture the way his eyes lit up when she said something clever, or the way his dimples hollowed when he laughed.

Or the way he looked at her. The silence shifted, becoming clearer, becoming something she didn't want to leave.

"Are we going to die?" she whispered, as if he had the answer.

Tether's gaze dimmed. He pulled back. She could feel him retreating behind his walls, away from her, donning his mask of cold apathy, one he hadn't worn around her for months. It felt wretched.

So she reached over the table and kissed him. She regretted it instantly, even though after a moment of surprise, he kissed her back. He cupped the side of her face with such tenderness, she could have been made of glass. She leaned into that touch.

She wanted it to last forever, this moment.

But something about it felt wrong. He held her like she was a lifeline and he was drowning. He kissed her like she was already gone and he was saying goodbye.

She stilled. As if he sensed her thoughts, he pulled away, letting his hand drop from her cheek. "I can't," he said, voice hoarse. "We can't do this." Something like disgust flared across his features, along with anger. Sadness.

"Did I do something wrong?"

He didn't respond. He wouldn't even look at her.

He stared down at the desk and began writing something like she wasn't standing right there, waiting for an answer.

She looked at him again, finally noticing how broken he was. She had seen it the day he told her about his parents. She had thought they were the same. But they weren't. She could separate herself from her ghosts. Her pain didn't define her. It waned over time, shrinking into a memory. Her pain lived in the past.

Tether's pain was different. He was tortured, consumed by his ghosts. His pain followed him everywhere. It grew and grew until it was the only thing he could feel. His pain lived within him; it became him, and he became it.

She left the library without looking back. She couldn't bear to witness his disgust or his anger and wonder what she had done wrong.

We can't do this. He was right. They shouldn't. The war was coming. They didn't have time for feelings that were doomed to die.

The next day, Tether was nowhere to be seen at training. Elaine tried to ignore his absence. But his desk was empty in Battle Tactics, too, and again in Wren's class. No one had seen him since the simulation yesterday. Elaine asked. Worry cemented itself in her chest when he didn't show up for the simulation that evening. Something was wrong.

She wasn't stupid or self-centered enough to believe he was avoiding her. No one ever missed class or didn't turn up for the simulation. Certainly, Tether would be the last person to, especially not for such a silly reason as a kiss. She sprinted to his room after the simulated battle ended. She knocked loudly on his door.

Nothing.

She tried to open it, but the handle blocked her. Locked. She hesitated. "Tether?"

Silence. If he were inside, he would at least tell her to leave. So she kicked the door open. Wood splintered around her foot.

The room was dark. She peered inside. "Tether?" she tried again.

No response.

She flipped on the lights. Her worry morphed into sinking dread.

His room was destroyed. Drawers were ripped off their hinges, glass from the lamp and chandelier shattered across the rug, clothes torn into ragged pieces. Gashes split open the mattress, foam stuffing spilling onto the floor. This wasn't a methodical job; it wasn't somebody looking for something. This havoc was the product of a breakdown.

Footsteps approached her from behind. For a moment, Elaine thought it was Tether. She turned around, mind warring between feeling relieved or scared to see him.

But it was only Arthur. "Follow me," he said.

CHAPTER 36

Follow me. Two words spoken with such gravity, Elaine didn't question the instruction. Two words acting like a leash—no, more like bait. Curiosity spurred her to trail behind Arthur, not force. She was the fish, and whatever Arthur was leading her to was the worm. By the tense set of his shoulders, it wasn't pleasant.

Moonlight spilled from the library windows, casting a pale glow over the dark wood and rows of leatherbound books. In another life, Elaine might have attempted to read them all.

Arthur tugged on the spine of the imposturous book, removed its neighbor and fished for the switch. Elaine heard a muted click, and the bookshelf unhinged from the wall. A draft of air escaped the secret chamber, freezing from being trapped so long in a tomb.

Elaine shivered. The hairs on the back of her neck rose. The Fall girl was dead. Tether had killed it to save her. She had watched the life drain from its eyes, the fight bleed from its body in black fluid. So why was Arthur taking her to an empty dungeon?

The shadows darkened as they crossed the hall. They stopped where Elaine knew a staircase spiraled down. Arthur retrieved a match from his pocket and removed a candle from the wall. The fire danced, rising and falling, an unsteady source of light. At times, Arthur's back blocked the glow, and Elaine had to feel for the next step in darkness. She lost her footing near the end, tumbling sideways. Her hand slammed into the wall for support. The rough stone grated against her palm. She took in a sharp breath.

Arthur had already reached the bottom. "Are you hurt?"

"No," Elaine replied, though she could feel the new scratches when her hand brushed her shirt.

Arthur's candle failed to illuminate the dungeon. There was something comical about the image, Elaine thought. A lone flame in a vast chamber of darkness. Trying and failing to fend off the shadows.

They approached a cell on the far end of a dungeon, to the right of the one that had held the Fall girl. Elaine glanced at the monster's old cage, which was empty.

"You know," Arthur started to say, catching Elaine off guard; he wasn't usually a conversationalist. "We thought Miranda Hane was the one who freed it. The dead girl?" he prompted, as though that would jog

Elaine's memory. As if Elaine didn't already know the dead girl's name.

"It turns out we were right."

Elaine blinked in shock. Miranda? The girl so concerned about protecting her mother from the Fall? "What reason could she possibly have to help them?" Elaine asked in disbelief.

Before Arthur could respond, another voice broke the silence, snaking through shadows. "I told you not to bring her." Words laced in hatred.

Elaine froze. She had forgotten about the cell—but more than the unexpectedness of another person was the jolt of recognizing that voice. She knew it well. It had taunted her, hurt her. Joked with her, encouraged her. Revived her. And the lips that spoke those words, she knew them well, too.

"Tether?"

No response, like he regretted saying anything and wanted to hide from her. Like he was guilty.

By the way Arthur's amber eyes flashed... She was right. It was Tether in that cell, Tether who didn't want to see her here. She took a tentative step toward the cell, then another, until she was close enough to wrap her fingers around the bars. The iron was cold, but Elaine barely felt the frosty sting. She searched for him, not knowing what she wanted to find.

There he was, cloaked in shadows where the light from Arthur's candle couldn't seem to reach. But she could make out the outline of his lean body pressed against the wall, as far from her as he could get. Elaine ignored the wrench in her chest. Her brain refused to put the pieces together.

"What's going on?" Elaine asked Arthur.

"As I was saying," Arthur said, picking up the threads of her conversation. "Miranda freed it before she was eliminated."

The night of the banquet. A memory of those moments struck Elaine like a blow to the head, and suddenly she was back in that stupid dress, spinning across the floor, laughing without a care in the world like she wasn't going to die in a year. With Tether. Dancing with him, dying with him. She supposed it was the same, in the end. Now meaningless.

"Except Miranda was doing the bidding of someone else. Someone with a vested interest in freeing the Fall."

Elaine hated that she glanced at Tether, and hated even more that he looked away.

"You see, Miranda wanted to protect her mother, and she saw the writing on the wall. Or the ranks on the wall, rather." Arthur chuckled at his own joke. "Once she was eliminated, she made a deal. Free the Fall, and she and her mother would be safe when the war finally came. Except, she realized too late that perhaps that promise was empty, so she came back. Didn't she, Tether?"

Again, Elaine stole a glance at his shadow, and again regretted it. This time, he held her gaze. Opened his mouth. To say what, Elaine would never know. But anything would have been enough. She would have swallowed whatever lies he fed her, happily. Because at least if she kept his lies, guarded them as truths, she could keep him, too.

But Arthur never let him speak, burying the words Elaine yearned to hear. "It's quite impressive, actually, that she managed to find her way back. Unfortunately, the Fall got to her before us. Poor girl."

Elaine remembered what Miranda looked like. Slashed skin, bite marks, bruises peppering her corpse. Poor girl couldn't begin to describe the savageness of her death.

Arthur shook his head, though the gesture felt insincere, like it was more for Elaine's benefit than any actual remorse he held. "But back to the matter at hand. Who convinced Miranda to do it?"

Arthur basked in the pause. His dramatics made her dizzy.

Who convinced Miranda to do it? Tether, for he was the one trapped in a centuries-old dungeon. He was the one whose silence screamed his guilt.

A growl escaped Tether, animalistic, raging. Vengeful. And Arthur smiled at it.

"Who, other than one of the Fall himself?"

CHAPTER 37

For a fraction of a second, Elaine's heart stopped beating. Her lungs stopped breathing. Everything—even time itself—simply stopped for that moment, like nothing existed outside her anguish. It was something more than disbelief, something more than shock, that paralyzed her. Betrayal. A betrayal that stung in the way no physical injury could, cutting so deep she was almost surprised she was still alive.

And as she broke into a million pieces, Tether just watched, lips pursed, silent. As if he were waiting for some sign that she didn't despise him with every fiber of her being. As if, after all his lies, there was even the slightest chance she could forgive him. Because that's what it all had been, in the end. So many lies stacked on top of each other that nothing about him, nothing between them, had been real.

She didn't bother asking Tether if Arthur was telling the truth. She could see it written across his face.

Perhaps something in her eyes gave away her heart breaking. "Elaine..." he said, but faltered. What could he say? *I'm sorry for spying, I'm sorry for lying, I'm sorry for working to murder your species. I'm sorry for making you believe you ever meant anything to me.*

But in this new silence, one marked by hesitation and betrayal and lies, she wondered if he even regretted it. He had always been skilled at masking his emotions; perhaps he relished in her despair, in having fooled her so completely.

"Elaine," he tried again, swallowing tightly. "I... I never meant to hurt you."

"Now that's not entirely true, is it, *Tether Nicolescu?*" Arthur drawled, speaking his name as a taunt.

Elaine inhaled sharply. In her daze, she'd forgotten they had an audience.

Tether snarled, baring his teeth. Arthur seemed to enjoy this, the ghost of a smile tugging at the corners of his mouth. "You *did* want to hurt Elaine. In fact, not only did you want to hurt her, you planned to kill her, isn't that right?" There was no hint of doubt in his tone, no room for Tether to deny the accusation.

Instead, he turned to Elaine, blue eyes pleading. "No—Elaine, I didn't think... if I had known it was you..."

"Known what was me?" Elaine snapped. She'd had enough of being left in the dark. She was sick of secrets.

"It's a shame," Arthur said, cutting off whatever Tether was about to say, "that it took us so long to figure out that Tether was our mole. If we had discovered him earlier, you might not be so upset, Eliane."

She faced Arthur then. His mouth was set in a frown, but the way one could read a smile not by the lips, but by the eyes, she failed to find the sentiment in his gaze.

"And bravo, Tether, for your performance killing a sister. You almost had us fooled. It must have been hard, to betray one of your own, even if it was only semantics."

Elaine thought back to the moment Tether had killed the Fall girl. It hadn't looked like a performance. He'd looked genuinely pertur—

She steeled her jaw in annoyance at herself. Here she was, falling for his tricks yet again.

Tether seethed from behind shadows, finally moving closer to the bars, closer to Elaine. She took a step back as the candlelight smoothed the angles of his face. He noticed her retreat, pain flashing across his face. Then he faced Arthur and his hands tightened into fists. "Don't act so innocent, Simovan. You've kept secrets from her, too," he fumed. "Why don't you explain to her what she is? What you made her into. Explain to her that she's just a pawn in your game, and that you never gave her a choice."

Arthur contemplated Tether's angered demand. He focused on Elaine. "I was going to tell you eventually, before you deployed, though I suppose now is as good a time as any. As you know, the Fall operate eusocially. At the center of this social dynamic is the queen. She influences the behavior of the hive. Without her, their species would be uncoordinated, ineffective at destroying planets. We have been fighting the Fall for millennia." He sighed, as if to punctuate that last point. "No matter how many times we've tried to stop them from killing, we've failed. They are too organized. The only way to truly fight them would be to level the playing field first."

Her mind halted, not fully understanding—and not fully wanting to. Arthur seemed to be waiting for her to say something.

Tether spoke instead. "He made you into a weapon, Elaine. You're his little *experiment*." The venom in his voice wasn't meant for her, but his words stung nonetheless.

"Experiment?" was all she could think to say.

Tether's voice came out softer this time. "You are your colony's queen."

Her colony's... queen. She turned over the phrase, as if searching for some meaning other than the obvious. Other than the truth, because she didn't know if she could face it. "What... what does that mean?" she asked.

"You are the key to ending the Fall's reign of terror, once and for all," Arthur said.

"No," she ground out. "What does this mean *for me*."

"It means people will gravitate towards you. It means that when you pursue a goal, those around you will pursue it with you, for you. It means that when it comes time to fight the Fall, you will be the reason for a united front. You will be the brain that commands the army."

Lines of confusion etched between her eyebrows. "I can... control people? How come I've never noticed it before?"

Arthur shook his head. "It's more nuanced than that. You can't control an individual, per se, not in the way you seem to be thinking. It's more that your will can guide the actions of a group." He paused, then added, "Perhaps you never noticed because you weren't looking. It's a subtle thing, this power. Besides, it will grow stronger soon enough."

Elaine searched through her memories for moments where this hive-mind effect may have occurred. When she was younger, she'd always gotten her way, she'd always had many friends; Lily was the only person she couldn't seem to get along with. But that was nothing special. More recently, however, there were instances that caught her attention. In the ring, she'd never gotten hurt, as if her opponents were always worried for her wellbeing. In the last trial, they had executed her idea perfectly, without question or much explanation. But even that could be chalked up to mere circumstance.

They had voted for her to stay.

But—grow stronger? That invited more questions, but she voiced the loudest, "How is this even possible?" *How could a person be made into a hive mind in the first place?*

Tether seemed curious, too, leaning forward ever so slightly. She hated that she noticed, that she was so attuned to him that she could detect the slightest shifts in his composure. His gaze slid to hers, and in that single, silent moment he told her a million regrets and all she could do was stare back.

"You were created in a lab—your DNA was altered so that you could grow into this role."

"My DNA..." She had never been able to find her biological parents. Helen and Evan would always freeze when she brought it up. Now she understood why. She didn't have real parents. "Did Helen and Evan know?"

"No," Arthur assured her. "We thought it better that nobody knew, even you, until absolutely necessary."

"Even me?" she scoffed. "You didn't think I had a right to know that aliens screwed with my DNA? What happened to your morals?"

If Arthur was offended, his expression gave nothing away. "It would have endangered you." He shot a pointed glance at Tether. "Trust me, Elaine, if we could have safely let you know, we would have. You deserve to know why you were created. But you also needed to survive."

She needed to survive. Something about the way he said it stripped her of her personhood and reduced her to a *thing*. A thing created under a microscope, a thing with the power to conquer evil. A weapon, as Tether had called her. But a thing nonetheless.

"Elaine, I never would have hurt you, never, I swear—"

"Stop, Tether." She squeezed her eyes shut. "Just... stop."

But he didn't stop. "I love you," he whispered.

She froze. He did, too, as if only realizing the weight of his words now that he had heard them aloud. The quiet crackling of Arthur's candle filled the dungeon.

Then a rage unlike anything Elaine had ever felt poured through her. It was strong; it was all-consuming. It was the aftermath of betrayal. She bit the inside of her mouth so hard it drew blood. The metallic tang rolled over her tongue. She took a calculated step forward. "Is this a game to you?" Her lips shook, even as she tried to calm herself. "You love me?" She laughed, bitter and angry and sorrowful. It sounded wrong, bouncing off the crooked stone walls of the dungeon. "You don't love me, Tether. You're a *monster*."

He flinched.

She couldn't help but add, "And I could never love you."

She wasn't sure if the flicker of hurt in his eyes was part of his act or if he truly cared. But she felt the tears finally starting, so she turned on her heel and left him to rot in the belly of the mountain.

CHAPTER 38

Helen used to wonder if there was something wrong with Elaine. Her daughter never cried. Not when she scraped her knee falling off a swing, not when Lily stole her toys, not even when she got lost in the forest behind her house until midnight when Evan finally found her.

Lily's death was the first time Elaine had ever shed a single tear, and she quickly discovered she hated crying. She hated the feeling of trying to blink the liquid away only for it to slide down her cheeks relentlessly. She detested the way her shoulders would cave in and her chest would shake as sobs wracked her body. After that, she vowed never to cry again. And it seemed like an easy enough promise to uphold. Only Lily had ever deserved her tears, and it wasn't as though her sister could die a second time.

Yet, as Elaine fled from the dungeon, a warm tear fell onto her cheek and left a disgustingly wet trail across her flushed skin. Then another followed. One for being fooled, and the second for discovering that her life didn't entirely belong to her, but to a cause.

Helen had been right, after all. There was something wrong with Elaine, it just wasn't anything to do with crying.

Genetic mutant. Freak. Weapon.

She scaled the staircase up to her rooms. She wanted to lock herself inside and not come out for days. Or weeks. Or simply stay in there forever. Though she knew that wasn't an option—they *needed* her, she snarked internally, mimicking Arthur's voice.

But she didn't care. They could need her all they wanted, but she needed space. She needed to be alone, to think. To process.

She skipped training the next day. She missed class, and then missed the evening simulation, too. She refused to leave her room even to eat.

Who am I?

She didn't know anymore. She'd grown up—as most children did—with the belief that she could be whoever she chose to be. Now she knew she'd never had a choice.

Who am I?

A daughter of none, born to the careful calculations of gene editing. A girl of purpose, wielding a power that could save her species.

Who am I?

Elaine Carter, a weapon whose fate had been stolen long ago.

Her power scared her. She didn't understand it. She couldn't fathom how to use it. And the hive mind seemed to operate independent of her consciousness, influencing others whether she wanted it to or not. She had the creeping suspicion that she would never be able to control it. That the Simovans had planted within her an ability that simply *couldn't be controlled.*

A knock rapped at the door, wrestling her from her thoughts. She contemplated not answering it.

"Elaine?" Mason.

She crawled out of bed and opened the door. When she passed the mirror, she saw a stranger.

"Are you okay?" Mason studied her with concern.

"Fine," she said. "I'm fine."

Her words had little effect. She couldn't even convince herself. "You weren't in class. I thought something happened," he said.

"Nothing happened."

He saw straight through the lie. "We were all worried."

Because I'm a hive mind! The urge to scream crawled up her throat. Nothing was real—not their worry, not Mason's kindness, not Tether's love. Nothing had ever been real.

"I'm fine," she repeated, hoping he would leave, but her voice cracked.

"Elaine," he said softly. "You can trust me. You know that, right?"

She almost told him to leave. But the thought of being alone, trapped in her head hating herself, made her say, "Do you want to come in?"

They took up opposite sides of the sofa. "What's wrong?" His tone was soft, accepting.

She shut her eyes before answering. "Yesterday I found out that I—" she took a steadying breath. "I'm a hive mind."

Mason's brows furrowed. Then he understood. "Like the Fall."

She nodded, biting her lip. Would he hate her? She would. She would hate the idea of surrendering her will more than she hated influencing others'.

"And we're all... part of the hive?" he asked.

"Arthur says it's the only way to beat the Fall," she said.

"How is that even possible?"

She fidgeted. "Genetic engineering. Aliens screwing around with human DNA."

He let out a long exhale. "Well, I didn't see that coming. I mean, it makes sense, I guess, but..." He leaned into the couch with a dumbfounded expression.

"Yeah."

Neither of them spoke for a few minutes. Then Elaine asked, "Why were you at the dungeon that time?"

"Oh," he said, as if recalling a distant memory. "I saw Miranda go down there after the banquet. I was curious. But there was nothing there."

"That's because she freed the Simovans's prisoner."

"What?" Mason's eyes went wide. "What prisoner?"

Elaine explained that the Simovans had kept a Fall locked up beneath the castle, and that Miranda had set it loose at Tether's request. She also mentioned that Tether was a Fall.

Mason's mouth hung open by the end. "No way. I always felt like there was something off about him."

Elaine had, too, but she had ignored her instincts. She had mistaken her unease for something else.

Mason seemed deep in thought. "You remember when you asked where I learned how to use a gun?"

She nodded.

"The reason I didn't want to talk about it was because, I..." he ran his hands through his hair in obvious agitation.

"You don't have to tell me," she said quickly. "You don't owe me an explanation." She regretted ever doubting his loyalty when she had so easily trusted a traitor.

"No, no, I want to." He smiled, and though it was strained, she smiled back. "I'm not proud of where I come from. Back home... I was part of a gang." He peered at Elaine to gauge her reaction. Whatever he saw—acceptance, imprudence—encouraged him to continue. "I did things I'm not proud of. I'm good at beating people up because I did that a lot. I'm good with guns because I did that a lot, too. My family got killed when I was little, and I had to watch out for myself. If I hadn't joined... Well, I didn't really have much of a choice.

"That invitation was my ticket out. And a chance to do something good for once. I felt bad a little at the beginning, because I didn't have a family I needed to protect or anything like you guys did. I felt guilty, and... ashamed. We're supposed to be the crusaders, you know—fighting evil and saving the world and all that. But I've done so much evil, inflicted so much pain, that it feels wrong for me to be here. I feel like I'm pretending to be something I'm not."

We're all pretending to be something we're not, Elaine thought.

"You can't control where you come from," Elaine said. *Or what you're born as.* As she spoke, she realized it wasn't only Mason she was talking to. "All you can control is what you do. That's what really matters. And we're going to save the world."

CHAPTER 39

"Using gravity assist, your rocket will reach the first base within a week," their physics professor explained. An image of the Simovan rocket was projected on the board. Even without scale, Elaine could tell it was gargantuan.

Ava tilted her head at the drawing. "Why are we all traveling in the same ship?"

"That decision was made by the Simovans," the professor said plainly.

"We should ask for multiple ships so we can split up," Ava went on, undeterred. "It doesn't make sense to put us all together. That makes it too easy for the Fall to eliminate us before the battle even begins."

"It's like designated survivor," Gino quipped. "Gather all the important people together, and boom!"

The professor raised his eyebrows at that. "If you'd like, you may bring up this suggestion to the Simovans. My job is to educate you about your flight and your vessel. Please let me do my job."

They went quiet again, refraining from pointing out the flaws in the plan which seemed to multiply with each passing day.

For one, as Mason pointed out, they didn't have nearly as much experience organizing troops as senior military tacticians. One year of classes couldn't make up for that, especially when half of the lectures before the trials had nothing to do with battle.

A more concerning flaw that Gino mentioned was that the schematic showed that the majority of the ship's energy was being diverted to propulsion, not nearly enough left over for armaments, and even then there were inconsistencies. A mere ten percent of their energy was dedicated to a similar propulsion mechanism as their trial ships, and eighty-five percent was devoted to some sort of compact collider.

"I tried to ask about the collider," Gino said. "But he wouldn't tell me anything. It was so weird. I mean, it has all the bits of the large hadron collider with magnets and the accelerator, but..." He paused, as though debating if he should say something.

"What is it?" Ava asked.

"I mean, I'm not sure," he prefaced, "but I think it's some sort of wormhole generator. Like if you collide elementary particles fast enough, you might be able to generate a very small black hole. Black holes bend space time... It's never been done before—well, by humans at least, so I really don't know."

The Simovans supplied them with little more than the most basic information—about the enemy, about the timeline, about the troops they would command, about the technology—and expected them to charge into battle blindly.

Then again, it wasn't as though they had any other choice.

———

The ghost-woman was waiting outside Elaine's door when she returned from class.

"Come with me," she said dully.

Elaine obliged, following the ghost-woman upstairs. She crawled through the passage into Arthur's office.

He was sitting behind his desk when she dropped onto the floor. "I understand you might have questions," he said.

She had many. But first, "How is it even possible that a Fall infiltrated our ranks?"

Arthur propped his elbows on the desk. "Like I said earlier, the Fall continue to advance. They managed to supplant a Fall consciousness into a human body."

"They supplanted... So Tether *was* human?"

"Yes. He has been human for the past eighteen Earth years." He leaned forward, as though excited to say, "I have a theory about him, and you. Would you like to hear it?"

She nodded.

"I theorize that you were slowly pulling Tether into your hive. That would explain why he did not kill you," he said. "Fascinating, isn't it? You are stronger than I predicted. What a surprise! And I am not often surprised."

Elaine swallowed the lump in her throat. Fascinating.

"You see, we had known there was a Fall among you since the start of the trials. Our prisoner, since she was detached from her hive, was essentially brain-dead. You can tell by their eyes. Their pupils darken and expand to fill their entire sclerae when they are disconnected from the hive mind. However, she started to act more alive once you humans arrived, which led us to suspect one of you was a Fall. Of course, we were right."

Elaine shifted in her seat, suddenly annoyed. "Why didn't you get rid of him in the beginning? Why wait? If I'm so important, why leave my would-be assassin alive?" The logic behind Arthur's decisions continued to confuse her, never mind that his motives were as clear as the mountain's fog.

"I'll tell you something no human yet knows, Elaine." He smiled conspiratorially. "Among Simovans, certain gifts allow us to tap into the universe's energy. I happen to possess the gift of someone you might call a seer."

That piqued her interest. "You can see the future?"

"No, it is not so simple a craft. I cannot *see* the future in the same way you cannot see in every direction with one set of eyes. The future is composed of many threads, many possibilities, all splitting off into infinite other ones. In short, there is no *one* future to view. My gift is to differentiate between those futures with low potential of actualizing, and those that are more likely to pass. I can understand how certain decisions may impact the likelihood of those futures. For example, I could see, even before knowing that Tether was the Fall we searched for, that he would not kill you." He paused, letting his explanation sink in. "I allowed him to live in anonymity because I was curious to see what would happen if I didn't interfere."

She bit back a retort about whether or not her foolish heart had satisfied his curiosity. "Are we going to win the battle? Can you see who will survive?"

His mouth curved into a knowing smile, the one that told her not to trust his answer. "All will be well. That is what I can see."

Elaine thought that was the most useless gift in the world if it produced answers like that, but she sensed he wasn't telling her everything.

"Can the Fall speak through minds?" she asked.

He nodded. "Some more than others. Tether is naturally quite strong in that regard, from what I have observed. Which is most likely why he was chosen for his role."

His role to find and kill the hive mind; to find and kill Elaine.

"Is that all?" Arthur asked.

"One more thing," Elaine said. "Why did you have us vote as a final trial?"

Arthur fell against his chair, watching her closely. "What do you think?"

She drummed her fingers on the arms of her chair. "Because you wanted to test the strength of my ability. You wanted to see if the hive responded to having a hive mind."

A smile was his only response.

So she was right. The voting had been a trial in disguise. A trial just for her. She couldn't help but wonder what would've happened if she'd failed.

She returned to her room pensive. During the simulation, she was distracted, and perhaps as a result, they performed poorly. She couldn't stop thinking about Tether, and about Arthur's theory.

As if punishment for her thoughts, she heard him in her mind again.

Elaine.

CHAPTER 40

E*laine.*

His voice caressed her, so unlike the rasp that had first spoken to her.

She pulled the covers to her neck and tried to block it out. She shut her eyes and whispered to the darkness, "It's not real. It's just your mind messing with you. It's not real."

Elaine, he said again, as though he wanted to say more.

Elaine, I would like... to explain. He sounded weak. She told herself she didn't care. *I owe you... that much.*

He was a liar, and he was the enemy; he didn't owe her anything.

Go to our... spot, Elai—

His voice cut out. She felt his presence leave her mind, more abruptly than it ever had. She felt his shock.

She tossed and turned for the rest of the night, barely catching a glimpse of sleep. And when she did dream, she heard Tether calling out to her, over and over.

Sometime before the sun rose, Elaine made up her mind to visit Tether in the dungeon. She would push aside whatever gnarled feelings had obscured his deceit before and try to pry truths from him. After all, Tether was a Fall. If anyone knew the Fall's plans, it would be him.

She decided to test Arthur's theory. If Tether *had* enveloped into her hive—if he truly loved her, as he said— then he would tell her everything.

Elaine slunk into the library after the simulation, careful not to make a noise. She paused at the bookshelf. It was open. That gap meant one of two things. Either somebody had visited last night and forgotten to close it, or someone was currently down there. Both thoughts made her pulse race. She kept her footfalls soft as she descended the stairs, flinching when a pebble skittered. The sound bounced off the cramped stone walls. She waited until it faded into nothing, breath held.

Then she entered the dungeon.

"Tether?"

He stayed silent as she approached.

"Tether, I'm sorry." A lie.

She was not sorry. She was still reeling from his betrayal. She was still sorting through the tangled feelings choking her heart, cycling through anger, sadness, regret, bitterness, grief, longing, then back to anger again. She could never forgive him.

You're a monster. She had meant every word. He was a monster. Believing that made lying easier.

"I forgive you, alright? Can we please talk?"

Still, he said nothing.

Was he angry? He hadn't sounded angry last night, though Elaine was no expert at reading emotions telepathically.

"Tether, come on. Let's talk."

His silence unnerved her. With each second that ticked by, her annoyance grew. How dare he be angry at her? He had no right—

Her breath escaped in a mangled cry. Her hands flew to her mouth. Her eyes widened into dark wells of horror.

Tether wasn't angry.

Tether was dead.

CHAPTER 41

One day before deployment, Elaine prayed for the first time in her life. She fell onto her knees and brought her hands together. Her palms were sticky with sweat from her evening run. She closed her eyes and tilted her head to the sky.

"Please," she murmured under her breath. "Please be with us."

She remained in that position for a long while, unmoving, unfeeling. The breeze wandering in through the open window curled around her, a cool veil draping over her sin.

For those moments, she saw nothing but the black behind her eyelids.

But in that darkness she saw him. His body, slumped against the wall. His blood, running in one line down his forehead. The bullet hole, precisely centered above his eyes.

Her eyes flew open. She stood and began pacing the room. Her fingers twitched at her sides. She tried to shake the image from her mind to no avail.

She couldn't unsee it—couldn't unsee him.

For the past months, he had haunted her every waking moment, and then followed her into her dreams, too. She wished she could erase him from her memory. Wipe his smile, his laugh, his touch, his gaze, from her brain.

But most of all, she wished to stop reliving the moment she discovered him dead. She had cried all night.

She had almost thought she might have forgiven him one day, if she survived the war and humanity destroyed the Fall. A stupid, grief-stricken thought she had banished immediately.

She steadied herself. Tomorrow she would leave Prysnen. She would leave Earth.

"You will be ready," Arthur had said to her last week, when she expressed concern that her powers hadn't yet strengthened. "I promise that when the time comes, you will be ready."

The time had come, and she was not ready.

She was not ready.

Her power barely manifested. She could hardly notice the effect of her influence on the others any more than she had before. Weeks passed without change. Her ability refused to grow as Arthur assured her it would.

And even if a great power did magically appear tomorrow or on the eve of battle, she wouldn't have a clue how to wield it. Arthur wouldn't teach her. He'd only given one of those knowing looks and half-answers when she'd asked him to.

One day left. Hours counting down to deployment. Without thinking, Elaine went downstairs to the library.

The door creaked as she pushed it open. Even though the moon basked the library in a silver flush, Elaine no longer saw magic in this room. She had not stepped foot inside since Tether's death. But today she did. She walked through the stale air toward the reading nook tucked behind a wall of books. She held her breath. *Our spot.* Her heart clenched. A letter sat expectantly between the pages of the book Tether had left on the desk.

A delicate layer of dust hugged the fabric of the cover. She swept it off, ignoring the way her hand shook. The envelope fell from the pages onto the desk. In navy ink, written with the utmost care: *Elaine Carter.*

She opened the envelope and unfolded the paper.

> *Dear Elaine,*
>
> *If you are reading this, I am most likely dead.*
>
> *Before you throw this letter away or burn it out of hatred for me, please let me explain. You don't have to love me. You don't even have to stop hating me. Just let me talk to you one last time, in the only way I can. Please.*
>
> *When I first saw you, that day you arrived at the castle, you looked so lost. You were drifting, alone and hurting. I could tell. It was ironic, then, that in that moment I was found.*

Not once in my life had I ever felt anything. Like I told you, I was as numb emotionally as I was physically. But when I saw you, I felt alive for the first time. My heart sang to be near you. I should have known then, what you were. I think a part of me did, but I didn't want to believe it. I craved you like a drug, and I hated you for it. I hated you with every fiber of my being.

You were a weakness. I wanted you gone—I needed you gone. That's why I tried to have you eliminated. I knew you hated seeing pain. I knew you would try to help me despite your better judgment. I saw it in your mind, that weakness. Remember the first time I spoke to you through your subconscious? You have the most beautiful mind, I don't know if you know that.

But you weren't eliminated, even though you should have been. The Simovans wouldn't let you get eliminated, their precious little hive mind. All the signs pointed to you, but I ignored them.

At one point I thought there was a chance Ava might be the hive mind. People listened to her, and she looked like Lily did in that memory. She told me she had a younger sister. I clung to that information like a dying man clings to life. I wanted so desperately to believe it was her. Anybody but you. When you mentioned Henry, I was hopeful. A brother, you said, not a sister.

During the third trial, I was afraid to go down into the lake and ponder my greatest hope. Because my greatest hope was the extinction of the human race, the extinction of Simovans. Before you hate me for it, Elaine, you must know that it is my nature. I cannot help but desire the necessary destruction. I am only part of a whole, and my desires are not always my own. But when I slid my hand into that chest, I thought of you. Your face, your smile, your laugh, your kindness—you were my greatest hope. I detested myself for it.

I was weak to fall for you. You would be my undoing. I suppose, in the end, you were.

I ignored every sign until I couldn't anymore. Until I finally got into your mind again and saw you in your memories. The Simovans were distracted hunting for their prisoner; they weren't there to protect you. Ever since the first time I broke into your subconscious, they had been guarding you. But that night, they were gone. It was my only chance to be sure. I had to do it.

I could hardly breathe when I realized whose memory I watched. I was meant to kill you, Elaine. You are a threat to my kind. I should have killed you. I almost did once. You were sleeping. The moon lit your face. You looked so peaceful asleep. But I couldn't kill you. You had awakened something within me. Humanity, maybe. Whatever it was, I couldn't hurt you.

The Simovans's prisoner, she saw you for who you were that day in the woods. She knew you were the hive mind. She would have killed you regardless, for she was deranged from captivity. Do you know the Simovans had kept her caged for a thousand years, pumping her full of drugs to keep her alive? I digress. She was going to kill you, and I should have let her. If I couldn't do it myself, I should have let her protect our species.

But then I did the unthinkable: I killed one of my own to save you. And I didn't think, I didn't hesitate. I didn't even regret it.

I am supposed to want you dead. I am supposed to have unwavering loyalty to my kind.

Do you understand now? You broke me, Elaine. You ripped me from my hive and stole me into yours.

You made me human.

Another thing—about Lily. You shouldn't feel guilty about her death, about the way you felt. You are a hive mind. I believe Lily was one, too. I believe the Simovans made many hive minds. And as a hive mind, you would have instinctually wanted her to die. Not only that, you should have wanted to kill her. You should have tried to kill her by your nature. So, actually, you did love her. You loved her a lot. And she loved you, too.

But you can't always overcome your biology.

I told you I loved you, and you thought I was lying. You thought I could not love because I was a Fall. Because I was a monster. But I did love you. I loved you more than should have been possible, and more than I ever should have let myself.

Maybe I am a monster. Maybe I was born to be evil. But I want you to know that I tried to change. I tried to escape who I was. I fought so hard, Elaine.

I tried, and I'm sorry. For everything.

Goodbye.

CHAPTER 42

A narrow bus carried the thirteen soldiers through the countryside to a sequestered hangar tucked between the folds of rolling hills. Seven hours of absolute quiet passed, absolute but for the buzz of the air conditioning unit and the occasional snort of the engine.

Elaine leaned into the headrest, staring up at the curved metal ceiling and every now and again glancing out the window. She didn't know what to think or how to feel when the gargantuan structure of the hangar came into view. So she didn't think, didn't feel anything other than her fingers drumming on her thigh.

The third of July—her last day on Earth. She sucked in a small breath and shook away the thought as the wheels slowed. The bus halted a few yards away from the entrance. They left the bus in the same manner they had boarded and ridden, stoic and quiet, lost in thought. She offered the driver a tight smile in thanks, and he dipped his head as though to salute her. As though to say goodbye.

In the week leading up to the takeoff, Elaine had seen goodbye everywhere. It was there when the sky cried for her, perhaps the last time she would see rain. It was there when Wren could barely look at their faces without pursing her lips sorrowfully, probably imagining them dead in the cold emptiness of outer space. It was there when Elaine noticed her reflection in the window; she still looked like a child, with her full cheeks and wide eyes. She would die looking like a child.

No, she wouldn't just die *looking* like a child—she would simply die a child. Her death would be stained by youth.

All of their deaths would.

Sometimes she forgot how young she was. It was easy to when the responsibility of going to war made her contemplate death so often. The young weren't supposed to think about dying.

Even the wind howled for them. Elaine glanced up at the pale blue summer sky for the last time, then stepped into the hangar. Sturdy beams held the building together, stripes along the wall slanted to form the roof. In the center of the space was their ship. It was a slender, jet-like thing, though at the moment, propped by towering metal rafters it looked more like a building. Reinforced glass windows winked at the somber-faced soldiers as they climbed the staircase choking the rocket to the elevator.

"Well," Mason said once they reached the top, a wide platform that led to the ship's hatch. She studied him.

Goodbye was written in the way he smiled—sadly and with great effort. She realized with a pang it was most likely the last of his smiles she would see. "I guess this is it."

She didn't know what to say other than, "I guess so."

Ava tsked at their exchange from beside the hatch. "Don't speak like that," she chided, though the hollowness of her words let them know she felt the same way. "You'll jinx us. Have a little faith, will you?"

Moments like these made Elaine wonder if the Simovans had made a mistake choosing her. She wouldn't describe herself as shy—reserved, maybe—but she also wasn't the type of person to tell others to keep their chins up in the face of disaster. Despite her destiny, she wasn't a natural-born leader like Ava. And… she still couldn't feel her power.

Sure, the others *tended* to flock to her, and they *tended* to look for her for instruction, but that was nothing worthy of her role—certainly nothing that would lend them an upper hand in battle.

"I don't feel ready," she whispered to Mason, the only one who would understand what she meant.

Could Arthur have overestimated his ability to edit her genes? The question had been nagging at Elaine for some time, but now it was more urgent.

"There's still time," he said, trying to sound reassuring, though his expression didn't convey the same hopefulness. If the Simovans placed such importance on her being a hive mind, did her frailty foreshadow their demise?

Mason was right, there was time—a week until they reached the base, and another until the battle was predicted to begin—but she doubted it would be enough.

The hatch slid into the rocket to allow them entry, and the hiss it made sounded like a warning: one last chance to turn back. But nobody heeded the pounding desire to run. Either they would die up there or die down here, and what difference did height matter to a dead man? At least up there they had the chance to fight. For themselves, and for their species, and for every species the Fall would slaughter after if they lost. As they boarded, the roof opened to the sky.

The interior of their ship was bare, their seats fastened to the smooth white wall across from the entrance. All the controls were on the level above, and the foodstuff and weapons and tools were on the floor below.

Elaine pulled the various seatbelts across her body. *Click. Click click click.*

Somewhere in deep space, the Fall gathered. Somewhere in deep space, humanity would make its final stand against something none of them fully understood, even after dozens of lectures about their enemy's psyche. The Fall were perverse, twisted creatures. Monsters. They ravaged and devoured. Their crusade left no survivors.

Elaine had long ago given up trying to make sense of the Fall's malevolence. They were evil, plain and simple. Attempting to comprehend the depth of their monstrosity was like wondering why a starving crocodile was sinking its teeth into your flesh. You were better off killing the crocodile and thinking later.

Reaching over from the seat next to her, Mason squeezed her hand. *It'll be okay,* the gesture was meant to say. But it felt empty, one helpless trying to console another in the face of great danger. It didn't make Elaine think it would be okay at all.

I should be the one trying to console him, she thought bitterly. *Hive mind and all.*

The rocket began to shake.

———

Once they cleared the exosphere, they had one day before the engines would shoot the rocket toward relativistic speed. Halfway through that day, it dawned on them that something was terribly wrong. This realization began as a trickle, the slightest unease manifested in raised neck hairs, but ended with the force of a dam breaking, horror in the wide-eyed silence.

It all started when Gino came down from the control room and said, "I think we're going the wrong way."

Elaine tore her gaze from the porthole.

"What makes you think that?" asked Ava.

"You know how the news was talking about where the Fall are coming from?"

"The stars that make up Orion's belt," Ava said.

Gino nodded. "Yeah, well, we're not going that way. I'm pretty sure we're going in the opposite direction."

"*Pretty* sure?" Beatrice pressed.

Gino pursed his lips. "One hundred percent positive, all right? I went over all the calculations."

"You took into account gravity assist?" Jace asked.

Gino looked offended. "Of course I took into account gravity assist."

Everyone turned to Elaine, whether they realized it or not. They went quiet, angling their heads toward her or shifting in their seats so they faced her or simply glancing in her direction. Something a person could easily miss if they weren't looking for it.

"Okay," Elaine drew out, still thinking. "*If* Gino is right, and we are heading in the wrong direction... We should contact the Simovans. They'll tell us if something's wrong. They'll tell us how to fix it."

Everyone nodded in agreement.

Elaine climbed to the control room, followed by Ava and Gino. She pressed the blue button that switched on their communications line to Prysnen.

"Hello?" she asked. "This is Elaine. Can you hear me?"

After a moment of static, the ghost-woman's voice rang out from the speakers. "Yes."

"Are we going in the right direction?"

"Yes."

Before Elaine could relax or anyone could roll their eyes at Gino, Arthur spoke. "Elaine, please have everyone return to their seats so I may speak to you alone."

Ava narrowed her eyes at the instruction but climbed downstairs without protest, Gino close behind. The hatch shut automatically behind them.

"You are alone," Arthur said.

"Yes," she confirmed.

"I would like to explain to you our decision."

She didn't like the finality of his tone. She stayed quiet.

"You must understand that the Fall cannot be beaten as things lie. To send you into battle against them, no matter how prepared, no matter how much you wished to fight, would have been suicide. You were right: you are not ready. You are not strong enough. The Fall would have won."

Would have? She stayed quiet.

"Even with a hive mind, humanity may not be strong enough for centuries. You are the first of your kind, Elaine. While you may not be the one to destroy the Fall, one of your descendants will. You will still be the reason humanity survives. Even if it is not in the way you thought."

Your descendants. She stayed quiet.

"In about two months, the Fall will arrive at Earth. They will destroy Earth." He paused. She stayed quiet. "They will destroy all humans on Earth. But humanity will survive because *you* will survive. It was the only way."

The blue light turned off and Arthur's presence disappeared.

You will survive.

She screamed.

CHAPTER 43

107 LIGHTYEARS FROM EARTH

The rocket finally slowed after two weeks of traveling just below lightspeed and one week tunneling through three wormholes.

It did not slow at the base, which they now understood did not exist. It never had. The base was a facade, as was the battle, something to lure them into this journey. A mirage that flickered when you looked at it too hard, oasis transforming into bleak desert. The promise of a last stand turned into the iron grip of a long life undeserved.

The rocket approached a vibrant purple planet. The planet's gravity tugged them into its orbit, engines kicking in to steady the landing.

The rocket's inhabitants were silent during the descent. Purple clouds rose to meet them, a mauve haze that obscured the view. The sky was dark and murky, but the pale outlines of three moons shone through. In another life, Elaine might have marveled at the sheer possibility of visiting another planet—might've even found this new world splendid, its purple sky and many moons beautiful. Yet, in this life, she could not. She could not think or feel anything besides a gnawing dread. *Henry.* He would surely die. Eight billion people—they would surely die, too. An entire race of people, gone in the blink of an eye. Gone without a fight, without a sound.

Gone but for a small cluster of individuals on an unnamed planet in deep space, who wished with all their hearts they had died, too.

EPILOGUE

Prinţ Naevros qi-Patru opened his eyes to a crowd standing over his body. He opened his eyes for the first time in ten years, then blinked for the first time in ten years. Sat up. Stood.

Drak-Trei had spun around its sun, a top set in motion eons ago by some ancient hand, back and again, here and there, all while he slept, dreaming of another world.

He could hardly recall it now, what he had seen. Wisps of memories came to him fleetingly as he prepared to meet the queen and her Albine. Feelings, mostly. Hatred, desperation, vengeance. Yearning. He could see hazy images, too. But if he tried to concentrate on them, they disappeared, as though his desire to *see*, to understand, was a hand dissipating the mirage.

"Prinţ Patru," said a servant, interrupting his turbulent thoughts. She bowed, hands clasped behind her back, gray robe billowing as she straightened. "Her Majesty is ready for you."

He acknowledged the summon with a nod, and the servant drifted away, shutting the door with a hollow thud. He turned to the mirror and paused. His reflection stared back at him. There was something strange about it, even though he'd seen it his entire life. Even though it was *him*. The sharp face, black hair, slender build, those milky eyes—they were his. Wholly his. Yet Naevros felt an unsettling disconnect from the person in the mirror, as though laying eyes on a forgotten friend for the first time in decades.

No. Naevros banished the dangerous thought. He was himself, only tired. He needed to believe that, or else he might as well paint a target on his back for the Albine to aim at. The queen's favor could only shield him so long.

He glanced at his reflection once more before departing. What he saw stopped his heart. Black eyes stared back. Bright black eyes—the pure ebony of a lost soul. Panic clawed at his mind. But when he blinked again, his eyes were clear. Empty. Pure.

He took shuddering breaths to steady himself. He was tired, seeing things. That was all, he reassured himself. His telepathic journey had made him susceptible to delusion. He would regain his strength, and the hallucinations would stop. Until then, he would guard his weakness from prying minds.

He willed his heart to a steady beat and warded his thoughts before leaving his chamber. The Răstel looked as it always had. Naevros didn't know what he'd expected. For the rooms to move? For the halls to shift in his absence? The queen's primary residence was a maze of obsidian, dark, shimmering stone that exacerbated their paleness. Its spires reached for the suns, sharp as a warrior's blade. Crystal domes provided illumination where the sparsely placed glowstones failed to, though the crystal didn't let more than a faint wash of light in. The queen and her Albine liked it dark, so that was how the Răstel was.

Naevros collected his thoughts before knocking. He'd saved the important information, stored it somewhere in the back of his mind to access when he awoke. The difficult part of the mission was over. All he had to do now was recount his discoveries to the Albine and hope it was enough.

The doors rumbled open, two guards on either side. The queen angled forward on her throne when she saw him. She looked the same as he remembered, golden hair, golden eyes, ghostly-white skin. *Beautiful.* That last thought felt more like a memory than a current feeling, as though he was reciting it out of habit—*no.* He clenched his teeth. He had to stop thinking like this. He had to remember that his thoughts were not private here.

He bowed to his queen.

"Rise." Her eyes glimmered.

The Albine exchanged whispers between themselves. He recognized most of them, though a few were strangers. New warriors to replace the fallen ones. The queen had been busy, it seemed.

"Tell us, Prinţ." She didn't need to elaborate.

Naevros obliged, reaching into his mind for the information they needed. Searching for what lay in the dark crevices of his subconscious. A bead of sweat trickled down his forehead. He'd been chosen for this mission for his ability to read thoughts, both his and others', that far surpassed even some of the Albine. And he was more expendable than they were.

But he was tired, and these memories were well hidden. He'd selected very few to save, for the more he tried to, the more likely he was to be discovered. By the time he found the memories, he was shaking.

He held up a hand to signal to the queen and her court that he was ready.

Before he could explain the maps and intricate plans, an image ambushed him. He almost stumbled back. It was the face of a girl surrounded by stars. He had taken great care to conceal it before he died. *Why?*

Why, why, why? The question pounded in his mind.

Brown eyes, a soft smile. A laugh sweeter than anything he had ever heard before. With a start, Naevros realized the girl was smiling at him. Laughing with him. And in this memory, he was smiling back.

ACKNOWLEDGMENTS

I'm not quite sure where to start with this page. There are so many people I would like to thank, so many people who helped make this book possible.

First and foremost: thank you to my family. To my parents for always encouraging me in my passions, from gardening to writing a novel. Thank you for always allowing me to read as many books as I wanted and for being the most enthusiastic cheerleaders as I tumbled through the highs and lows of writing this one. To my brother and cousin, whose eyes I trusted to read my work before anyone else. Your quips at my typos made the proofreading process much more enjoyable. And to my friends, your excitement made me excited to see this project through.

Now for a longer (and perhaps more rambling) list of thank-yous. I am forever grateful to my teachers, past and present. From my elementary school days: to Ms. Tamayo, Ms. J. Torres, and Ms. Morrison, who taught me how to write. In middle school, I was lucky to be taught by Ms. Salzinger, Ms. Alexander, and Ms. Rodriguez. I was told I always had my nose in a book back then, so thank you for fostering my love for fictitious worlds. It was in Ms. Rodriguez's eighth grade English class I realized that writing was a skill to be mastered (we were reading a short story about a girl waiting by the telephone; nothing happened, yet my attention never strayed from the page.

I thought it was magic until I read Ms. Rodriguez's writing and realized the magic could be learned). Thank you for teaching me your magic. In high school, my history teachers (Mr. Caron, Dr. Ermer, and Mr. Allen) opened my eyes to the fascinating stories of our world. There was never a boring moment in Mr. Caron's class, who taught history like a storyteller. Mr. Allen's lessons have inspired many ideas for future books. To Ms. Sanchez, Dr. Heller, Mr. Natland, thank you for cultivating my love for the sciences. Some of the topics Mr. Natland teaches in his physics class are in this book, so an extra thank you for making some of the wild sci-fi sound a little more realistic. To the greatest advisor, Ms. Sanchez (again), for always being there for your students and giving the most thoughtful and uplifting pep talks. Your guidance unfailingly pointed me in the right direction. I truly got so lucky to have you as a teacher and advisor. And finally, a thank you to the English department at Ransom. To Ms. Alexander and Ms. Morgan for supporting *Inklings* and giving students like me a space to explore creative writing. To Ms. Anderson, for teaching me poetry and the beauty of lyricism. To Dr. Chuang, who taught me to analyze literature and uncover symbolism. And to Dr. Rhyner, who helped me rediscover my love for writing; without you, I'm not sure I would've picked up this book from where it had been sitting in its earliest stages of the first draft.

I am forever grateful.